THROUGH THE HAND GLASS

Through the Hand Glass

CHAD GUNTER

Acrasia Media

CONTENTS

This book is dedicated to my son, the inspiration for this story!
I love you, Son!

Through the Hand Glass
Published by Acrasia Media
Charlotte, North Carolina

This book is a work of fiction. The characters, events, and places portrayed are fictitious. Any similarity to real persons, living or dead, is coincidental, and not intended by the author, with the exception of the character *Captain,* who is the author's son.

Publisher's Cataloging-in-Publication data

Names: Gunter, Chad Eric Sr., author.
Title: Through the hand glass / Chad Eric Gunter, Sr.
Description: Charlotte, NC: Acrasia Media, 2022.
Identifiers: LCCN: 2022906326 | ISBN: 978-1-958202-01-2
Subjects: LCSH Private investigators--Fiction. | Down syndrome--Fiction. | People with disabilities--Fiction. | Mystery fiction. | BISAC FICTION / Action & Adventure | FICTION / Disabilities & Special Needs | FICTION / Mystery & Detective / Private Investigators | FICTION / Thrillers / Crime
Classification: LCC PS3607 .U68 T47 2022 | DDC 813.6--dc23

First Printing, 2022

| 1 |

Chapter 1: Connor Has a Blast

The shotgun blast was deafeningly loud. The pellets tore through the cheap, wooden door of the aged motel, as if it weren't even there, adding a spray of wood fragments and splinters into the mix of the tiny lead meteorites that were already punching their way into Detective Gellar's atmosphere. Fortunately, the assailant had been aiming low, and Connor received the brunt of the wood and buckshot mixture in his left leg, instead of the face or any vital organs. Connor's quick move to retreat, coupled with the force of the impact, left him sprawling on his back. In the short span of seconds, Connor had already had his hand inside of his dress jacket to retrieve his service pistol from his shoulder holster. Before he had even got his hand on the butt of his gun, the shabby, tattered door flew open, and a large, rough-looking man wearing grease-stained bluejeans, a matching bluejean vest, and black boots stepped through onto the breezeway. As he was walking, he operated the slide action on the pump shotgun, chambering the next round. He began ranting some expletives, as he lowered the gun and placed the end of the barrel against Connor's forehead. Connor did not continue reaching for his pistol, but remained motionless. "Say goodbye, pig!" exclaimed the assailant.

"Hey!" yelled a voice from further down the breezeway. The man with the shotgun twisted quickly, and began leveling the weapon in the direction of the interceding voice. "Goodbye, pig!" yelled the distant voice as he fired a volley of rounds at the assailant. Detective Bryson was an excellent shot. He was well known in the department as *The Man that Never Missed.* Although his stint in the military had not been long, while he was there, he had earned multiple medals and awards for his sniper abilities. Each of his multiple rounds found the assailant's torso, and the man released the shotgun. It clattered to the concrete breezeway floor, and he dropped like a sack of potatoes, right at Connor's feet. Detective Bryson rushed up to the assailant, gun still in hand, and checked the man's vitals. No restraints were necessary. The man was dead. He moved to Connor and began checking him out. "Hey, partner. How're you feeling?" asked Detective Bryson. "Daniel, I'm hoping that shock sets in soon because my left leg hurts like nobody's business." said Connor. "Well, buddy, I don't know if *lucky* is the right word or not because your leg does have some holes in it . . . but that's the *only* place I can find any." said Daniel. "Are you sure? Just the other day you said there had to be one in my head." Connor joked, nervously deflecting his reality. Daniel had removed his jacket and was tearing strips off of it, as he talked on the speakerphone of his cellphone. "Shots fired and an officer is down. We need backup, paramedics, the coroner, a meat wagon, the whole shebang . . ." Daniel said, giving the dispatcher the address and all of the pertinent details. After tearing away Connor's left pants leg, he began securing the torn strips from his jacket around his leg to help stop the bleeding. In the distance, the two detectives could hear the approach of the cavalry, as announced by the sirens. Daniel gripped Connor's hand, smiled, and said "You're going to be just fine, partner."

| 2 |

Chapter 2: From Healing to Reeling

An investigation was standard procedure under the circumstances that led to the death of the assailant at the motel. Detective Gellar and Detective Bryson had been canvassing the area, and questioning residents in an attempt to get some clues for the armed convenience store robbery that had taken place a day prior to their confrontation with the perpetrator. It was assumed that Connor simply knocking on the motel door was enough for the paranoid robber to think the detective was on to him. They had very little info to go on, as the night clerk could only describe the robber as a big man wearing a ski mask, and brandishing a gun. The store's security system had apparently malfunctioned, and nothing had been recorded. The only possible lead had been an anonymous call about a suspicious guest at a motel close to the robbery. They also assumed that when he peeped out and saw a man that looked like, well, a plain-clothes detective, he grabbed his shotgun and fired through the door. Connor was fortunate that he had fired a little prematurely when he had begun raising the shotgun. He was *extremely* fortunate that his partner had been at the other end of the breezeway. Connor's anxious mind thought that it seemed that there was too much serendipity in play. If the simpleton had just answered the door and answered a few questions, even with lies that couldn't be proven otherwise, or had not even answered at all, the shootings would have never taken place. The perp would have probably gotten away with the robbery. Anyway, the stolen money from the convenience store was found in his room. He had a shotgun that even CSI couldn't bring out the serial number on. He also had an old-style, flip-type burner phone. The burner had placed and received a few calls, but the calls were traced back to yet another burner phone. The burner phone in the man's possession was traced back to a local variety store. It had been purchased so long ago with cash, and their old-style video surveillance had already been written over. The suspect was dead. A gun was recovered. The convenience store money was recovered. Case closed. All's well that ends well. Only things were not ending all too well for Connor.

Even though one of the finest surgeons in the state of North Carolina had performed a miraculous job with Connor's leg, the damage was so extensive, his leg would never be the same again. Connor, who was 5'5" had always held his own when competing with his coworkers in sporting events at annual gatherings. He even prevailed against some of the bigger men, in challenges where size usually did matter. He had sandy-blonde hair, a mustache, and a pretty hard body for a 46-year-old man. The once, athletic and agile man was now unable to move faster than an average gait, and he had the limp to prove it. He had been on desk duty as soon as he was cleared to return to work. He did not like sitting out in the open, in the middle of the main office of the department, where everyone that went through the office encountered him. In fact, he hated it.

Once his cast was removed, and his broken bones and tissues had begun to heal up nicely, he started his physical therapy. His commanding officer, Captain Lester, also required him to do some psychological therapy, and eventually had him take a psychological evaluation, just as when he had first applied to the force. He had been driving a desk for over three months when he had decided it was well past time for him to get back to his real work.

Before Connor left for the day, he headed to the captain's office. The door was open, but Connor politely knocked on the frame before going in. Captain Lester looked up from a report he had been typing in on the computer. "Gellar, my man, how're you doing?" asked the captain. "I am doing much better, thank you, Sir." said Connor. "That's good to hear. Calling it a day?" asked Captain Lester. "Yes, Sir, but I wanted to come by and talk to you before I left." said Connor. The captain sat up a little straighter in his chair. "Sure, partner, what can I do for you?" asked Captain Lester, giving Connor his full attention. "Well, Sir, it has been over three months now since the incident. I'm doing great on my PT, and I know I move slower now, but I think I'm more than ready to get back into the field." said Connor.

Captain Lester shifted uncomfortably in his chair. "Are you not happy with your current assignment?" asked the captain. "No, Captain, I'm not. I guess I just wasn't born to be a desk jockey." said Connor. "Don't you think you need a little more time to heal and see if there are further improvements in that leg?" asked Captain Lester. "Sir, even though I'm still in physical therapy, I'm pretty much not going to heal any more than I have already. They did the best they could with my leg, but this is me now." said Connor. The captain's eyes seemed to be searching the room for the right words to say. He wasn't sure if he was going to find them. "Connor, do you really think you *should* work as a detective with that leg as it is? Have you thought about what might happen if you needed to run?" asked the captain. "I have thought about that, Sir. We're always paired up with a partner. Some laws protect people from physical discrimination, as I'm sure you are aware. I may *limp* faster than a few detectives we already have around here, no offense." said Connor, not wanting to argue with his superior officer. Captain Lester inhaled deeply and then exhaled loud enough that Connor could hear him. "You're right, Connor. You're absolutely right. There are discrimination laws in place, but I truly doubt you could pass the POPAT now. You are also right in the fact that we may have other employees that may find passing the POPAT again to be difficult, but it's not *their* fitness in question right now, is it? I'm sure you wouldn't want to make an issue about that. But there's more than just your leg, Connor. Your psych eval is not helping your situation. Our psychologist has highly recommended that you do not return to the field in the capacity to do work as an officer. The incident has affected you deeper than you realize, Connor, I'm sorry. I was hoping that under the circumstances that maybe you would either choose to remain on desk duty, or maybe look into something within the department that would be a better, more suitable fit. You have gone through so much, I just haven't wanted to tell you . . . and I guess I was hoping that maybe you were ready to find something else, too. Then when you received the evaluation results, it wouldn't matter that much." said the captain.

Captain Lester was a man's man who didn't take anything off of anybody. He had been with the force so long, he had been eligible to retire many, many years ago. He had passed on many promotions because he loved being the captain. Even being in his early sixties, and of much less stature than your average male, he had the prowess to take down many larger and seemingly tougher people. Connor, having worked under the man for eleven years now, also knew that you couldn't meet a better, more honorable man. Although the captain's revelation to him confounded him, he could also tell that under his gruff facade, it pained Captain Lester to tell him this information.

| 3 |

Chapter 3: There's Always Hope

It was not a cookie-cutter home by any means, but it was also much similar to your average suburbanite house one would find in Edmonton, North Carolina. Four bedrooms with a connected two-car garage, and the required white, picket fence. Edmonton was a nice city in which to live. It had a lot of the benefits and amenities of a bigger city, but still had that hometown feel of a small city. Connor pressed the garage door opener button on the device clipped to his sun visor, waited for the large door to rise, and then pulled into the garage. He closed the garage-door, and then headed into the house through the side door.

Although the kiss Alexis received from Connor when he arrived home was heart-felt, she could immediately tell something was wrong. Not one to beat around the bush, she asked. "What's bothering you, honey?" she asked with concern. "Is it that obvious? I've always tried to wear my heart *inside* my sleeve." he replied, forcing a smile. "Well, I don't just *see* your heart, I can *feel* it too." she said. Connor smiled, genuinely that time and sat down at the kitchen table. His wife was preparing supper. Alexis washed her hands and then sat down in the seat next to him.

Alexis currently had long, blonde hair, as it did change from time to time. She was slightly shorter than Connor, and of average weight, with just enough extra in all the right places, as Connor would constantly remind her when she seemed self-concious. She had a very pretty face with a clear complexion. "It's over for me as a police detective." he said flatly. Alexis' eyebrows furrowed. "Because of your leg? They can't do that." she said. "No, not just my leg. The shrink said that I shouldn't return to police officer duty. Or should I say, *highly recommends* that I do not return to police officer duty. I'm so miserable doing desk duty." Connor said with exasperation. Alexis looked into his eyes. "We can fight this." she said. "We probably could. We might even find loopholes to win. But the fact is, if that's how I'm viewed now, I don't think I even want to be there anymore . . . and I don't blame anybody. Although I think I would be fine with a good partner like Daniel, just as the captain said, I probably couldn't pass the POPAT now, and I'm not going to sham my way through a psych eval." he said. Alexis was quiet for a few moments, and then said "Is there anything else in the department that you would enjoy doing?" she asked. "Not really." he answered, bluntly. "So quit." she said.

Connor offered a partial smile to his wife. "I'm serious.

Find something else that you like to do *somewhere* else. My job at the university will support us for a while until you do." Alexis said. "I can't think of *anything* I'd rather do than be a detective. You know how I had told you that I had always dreamed about it as a kid, and then worked my butt off as a uniform until I finally made it." said Connor. "I know, dear, I know. Sometimes life throws us curve balls. We either have to hit one of them . . ." she said. ". . . or strikeout." he finished.

Connor, Jr., or Captain, as his dad had nicknamed him many years ago, came walking into the kitchen. "Matey!" he exclaimed when he saw that his father was home. Captain ran to where his dad was sitting and gave him a bear hug and a big kiss. Captain was twenty-two years old. Although he had Down syndrome, unlike the preconceived notions that so many people held, Captain was the spitting image of his dad, only with the subtle differences that many individuals with Down syndrome shared. He had slight epicanthic folds around brilliant, blue eyes. His ears, hands, and feet were just a little smaller than the average typical person of his height and weight. Captain had a big, strong upper body with tremendous strength. He had some gold medals to prove it.

"Hey, Captain!" exclaimed Connor. When Connor saw his son's bright eyes and smile, everything negative in his mind temporarily vanished. Another preconceived notion was that all of the DS population were all so loving. There was no doubt in his mind that Captain *was* the most loving person he knew. However, on the few occasions that he did get mad, you'd better look out. "Did you have a good day, today, buddy?" Connor asked his son. "Mm-hmm." he replied.

After another hug with Connor, Captain hugged his mom and with slightly broken English asked "What we have for supper, Mom?"

After dinner, Alexis and Connor watched a few of their favorite TV shows, while Captain either watched one of his favorite shows, or played a video game on his computer or one of the many other game systems he owned. Oftentimes, Captain would multitask and play a game and watch a video at the same time. During a TV commercial, Alexis said "What about becoming a *private* detective?" Connor looked at her with his eyebrows raised. "I'm not kidding. I know it's not exactly the same as a police detective, but I imagine it would be very similar. I would think that it could even be very satisfying for you. Although there are some cons, I can see many pros as well." she continued. "You know, you might be onto something. It's definitely a possibility. Thanks, honey." said Connor, smiling.

| 4 |

Chapter 4: You'll Never Know Till You Try

Although Connor was still somewhat depressed about his work situation, he also had a glimmer of hope for the possibility of a career change that could be a positive move for his situation. Normally, Alexis took Captain with her to her teaching job at the university, but today, Connor had called in and taken the day off. He was going to do a little research on how to become a private detective. Captain had elected to stay home with him since getting to spend a weekday with his dad was not very frequent.

Connor had always been an early riser, so he got up when Alexis did. After kissing her goodbye, he carried his cup of coffee into his office and turned on the computer. He tried to be quiet, so Captain could sleep in. He opened an internet browser and began researching the private detective requirements for the state of North Carolina. Using the internet, it didn't take very long to find them. He was pleased to find that he had already met all the requirements for becoming a private *investigator*, as was the preferred term, if you were not in law enforcement. His time as a police detective with the force would count as the minimal of 3000 hours, or three years of training. All he had to do now was to submit the required applications and forms to the Department of Justice. Once he has been accepted, the PI license was good for two years. To keep your license, you must attend a board meeting, and take a minimum of twelve credit hours of continuing education during the two years. It seemed that everything could be performed online, as most things could be these days. Connor went ahead and submitted all of the necessary documentation, along with paying all of the appropriate fees.

After Connor had finished all of his application work, he decided to load a relaxing game on the computer. While he was playing, Captain walked into the office. "Good morning, my buddy!" said Connor, hugging his son. "You ready for breakfast?" Connor asked. "Yep." Captain answered. "Alright, I'll get your morning medicine and breakfast." said Connor. Captain switched on his computer, which was right next to Connor's. They had their computers networked so they could play games together. Connor retrieved Captain's medicine and breakfast. Ninety-nine percent of the time, Captain had his favorite brand of yogurt for breakfast, along with some low-calorie chocolate milk or orange juice. Connor realized that he had not even had any breakfast, so he also got himself his normal staple of a cup of cereal in milk. Connor and Captain were as close as a father and son could possibly be.

Even though Captain's actual age level equivalent was somewhat less than his actual 22-years-of-age, Alexis had always reminded him that all people are different. As far as social maturity and interaction goes, Connor figured that his son had him beat. When Connor asked him "Son, would you like to play our game?" he wasn't really sure what the answer would be. There was a time when it was always Captain asking his father to play, but as he grew older and more mature, that happened less and less. Connor was happy when he responded "Yes, we make a good team!"

The game allowed them to be on the same team, complemented by "bot" companions, and "bots" on the opposing team. They could see each other on their own screens, as they fought their enemy in different game scenarios, using various weapons. They would look out for each other just as if they were real soldiers. They played up until lunch time, and using different strategies, had managed to win most of their matches, even on the difficult setting. After lunch, however, Captain was ready to move on to other activities, leaving Connor to himself.

| 5 |

Chapter 5: Depressive Suspension

Over the next several weeks, even though it was basically the doldrums, Connor continued to do computer work and paperwork as his desk duty at the police station. He had completed his PT, and although he had some improvement in his leg, it was negligible. From time to time, his old partner, Detective Daniel Bryson, would stop by to chat, as he had done right after Connor had returned to work. Connor could tell that Daniel would downplay his work activities. He supposed it was out of guilt. He had thought of just telling Daniel to quit tiptoeing around him, but then thought that maybe the talks were actually helping Daniel to cope a little bit, himself. Daniel had not just been his partner. He was probably his best friend. There were times, he felt as if they were brothers.

One afternoon, after most everyone else had left for the shift change, Daniel had stopped by to check on Connor.

Connor had confided in Daniel that he had received the results of his psychological evaluation, and that he had, indeed, failed them, being considered mentally unfit to return to field duty.

"Look, you can take that psych eval again. In fact, you and I both know what answers they're looking for to pass it." said Daniel. "Yeah, I know. But not answering truthfully, even though I know some of the questions are loaded, just doesn't seem right. We've known each other for a long time, and you know how much I had wanted to become a detective with the force . . . but I never really shared with you *just how much* I had wanted it. I just *couldn't* be happy being a detective knowing I was working based upon fraudulent answers on my psych eval. Besides, I'd never pass the POPAT with this leg, if they made me take it again." said Connor, sullenly. "You're a good man, Connor. Maybe too good. But, that's what makes you who you are. And that's why I've always trusted you with my life." said Daniel, as he affectionately slapped his hand twice on one of Connor's shoulders. One of the side room doors opened up, and they both looked in the direction of the sound.

"And look who I'm stuck with now!" exclaimed Daniel, jokingly, nodding in the direction of his new partner as she entered the room. The phrase *stuck with* was definitely a joke. Detective Rachel Harris was the most aesthetically pleasing person in the department. She had beautiful, long, black hair. Her complexion was flawless. She had brown eyes, but they were so bright that they almost seemed unreal. They also had that unique shape, with slight epicanthic folds similar to his son's, that was seen in many people of Asian descent. Her figure would make a swimsuit model envious. She was substantially younger than either of the two men. Connor often wondered why she had chosen to become a police officer, but as long as he had known her, he had never really gotten to know her well enough to ask her. Connor had heard not to let her stunning appearance give you any doubts of her abilities, as she was a remarkably good cop. With Connor out of commission, she had just recently been offered the position to fill in for him. At age 26, she was now the youngest detective on the force. This was a stroke of luck for Daniel, Connor supposed, although like himself, Daniel was also a happily married man. *But still, who wouldn't mind having her as a partner?* thought Connor.

Rachel smiled an affectionate smile for Daniel in response to his joking comment, as she walked toward him, but her smile seemed to somewhat fade when she saw to whom Daniel was speaking. Connor felt as if she even had to force the smile to remain. He could feel the awkwardness in the room. It was so thick, he wasn't sure you could cut through it with a chainsaw. Connor assumed Rachel may be carrying some guilt with the convenience of sliding into his vacant position, with the circumstances as they were. Connor could see Daniel uncomfortably grappling with the situation, as he had felt the veil of awkwardness drop as well. *It's not her fault.* Connor thought, as he quickly tried to dissolve the awkwardness. "Look, Rachel. I'm happy for you. With everything that's been going on, I don't think I've even congratulated you. Enjoy your career. You couldn't have been paired up with a better partner than Daniel." he said. The cumbrous situation lightened a little, but not as much as Connor had hoped. "You're right, Daniel's the best, Connor, thank you." said Rachel, still unable to hold Connor's gaze. "Well, Rachel, you ready to get out there?" Daniel said, taking the discomfort level down one more notch. Rachel forced a smile as she nodded. "We'll see you around, Connor." said Daniel, gently slapping him on the back. Rachel quickly raised and lowered her hand to Connor as a goodbye, then followed Daniel out of the department's front door. "Be careful out there!" Connor exclaimed after them.

Connor's sleep that night was broken and fitful. He couldn't shut his mind down from the many things that weighed heavily on him as of late. He still had not received anything back from the DOJ concerning his PI application. He realized that he was lucky to be alive, but he still couldn't shake the feeling of being less of a man now, with his "bum leg," as he had begun to refer to it. Although he was grateful to have his job, he was still as miserable as ever at the desk. Not only was the desk job unenjoyable for him, but it was also a constant reminder of what he had lost.

Connor woke up the following morning with Alexis shaking him. He jumped up to the sound of the nightstand alarm blaring at him. As many things that had happened to him in life to deprive him of a good night's sleep, this was the first time he had ever not been wakened by the alarm. "Thanks, babe. I didn't sleep well at all last night." he said. "I know you didn't, you kept waking me up, talking and flopping around." she said. "I'm sorry." he said. "It's okay, I know you have a lot on your mind right now." she said. Connor put his mind and body in gear and headed for the bathroom, so he could shower and get ready for work. Alexis normally would sleep another hour before she had to get up and get Captain and herself moving, but she got up, went to the kitchen, made Connor a cup of coffee and some toast. When he arrived in the kitchen, he was surprised at the sweet gesture of breakfast from his wife. He kissed Alexis, and she pulled him in and wrapped her arms around him. "Honey, everything is going to be okay . . . I know it." she whispered softly in his ear. Alexis felt some of Connor's pent up tension release. He almost always held in or hid his emotions that were dichotomously classified as negative, but when they released each other from their embrace, she saw his eyes were wet where he couldn't quite hold all of his tears at bay. "I'll happily support any decision you make." she said. He knew she was referring to quitting the department. He was absolutely not going to quit and leave all the financial responsibilities to his wife. He would suck it up and deal with it. "I know you would." he said quietly. He kissed her, and then walked down the hallway and went into Captain's room, where he was softly snoring. He kissed his grown son's cheek. Captain's snoring stopped briefly, as he smiled with his eyes still closed. His lips formed a kiss and then he slipped back to sleep. Connor grabbed his lunchbox, left the house and headed to work.

| 6 |

Chapter 6: Some Good News

Connor was one of the few people in the department that still brought their lunch. When he brought it as a detective, he would eat in the car, except on the occasions when Daniel had asked him to eat at a particular restaurant with him. Now, he just ate at his desk. He knew a lot of his coworkers also used their lunchtimes as a temporary escape from the office. As unhappy as he was with his job now, he knew it made little sense to leave and then come back, especially having brought his lunch. The job would still be here, whether he left or not. As was his lunchtime routine of personal time use, he would use his smartphone and return personal calls and texts, read personal emails, track expected package deliveries, pay bills, and a host of other chores. He was amazed at the fact that these small devices could do just about anything these days. Connor's heart leapt as he was scrolling through the inbox of one of his email accounts. One of the email messages was from the Department of Justice. He quickly placed his finger on the email, opening it. It was official. All of his paperwork had been in order and everything had checked out. He was now a private investigator!

The remainder of the day seemed to drag on forever, although his spirits were high from having received some positive news for a change. He wanted to tell Alexis and Captain, but he wanted to tell them in person. When his coworkers that worked in the building had returned from lunch, he wanted to scream out "Guess what, guys? I'm a private investigator!" Not only did he want his family to be the first to know, he was still unsure of exactly what he was going to do. He could no longer concentrate well, and although he wasn't being held to any strict standard of production in the job he was performing, he certainly knew he wasn't getting as much paperwork done this afternoon as he had this morning. He was thankful when quitting time for his shift rolled around.

This time, Connor had found Alexis in the living room, sitting on the couch, reading a newspaper. They greeted each other with a kiss, and then Connor sat down quietly in his recliner. Alexis continued reading her paper. Just as before, she knew something was out of the ordinary. But just like other people that have expert intuition would know, she could tell from Connor's demeanor that something pleasant had happened for a change. After a couple of minutes of reading the newspaper, she finally looked up. "Okay, Connor," she said, using his first name, teasingly, as if she was upset with him. "out with it. I can sense that you are about to explode." she finished. He smiled and said "Let me call Captain in here." He shouted for his son, as Captain usually had the volume of whatever devices he was using turned up loudly. After a moment, Captain walked into the living room. As soon as he locked eyes with his son, the greeting that never got old, came from Captain's mouth: "Matey!" His eyes lit up, and so did Connor's. "Hey, my handsome guy!" said Connor. Captain gave Connor a big squeeze, then sat on his knee. Captain had been too big for sitting on his dad's knee for a long time now, but Connor never complained. Well, at least until his leg went numb.

"Family . . . you are now looking at a licensed private investigator!" exclaimed Connor. Both Alexis and Captain were very excited with his news. Captain gave his dad a hug. Alexis stood, rushed to the two men and wrapped her arms around both of them. "I'm so proud of you!" exclaimed Alexis. Captain already knew and understood what Connor's police detective job was. He also understood that now, his dad was a detective "on his own," like a character in one of his favorite video games. Captain had heard someone in one of the games refer to a character as the world's greatest detective.

After dinner, the Gellar's enjoyed one of their favorite shows, though Captain enjoyed his in the office, and Connor and Alexis had theirs in the bedroom. "So, did you tell them?" Alexis asked. "Tell my department about becoming a PI? No, not yet. I had wanted to tell you guys first. Besides, I'm not even sure exactly what I'm going to do now. There's probably a lot involved in the start-up of a PI business." said Connor. "I wouldn't think there would be that much at all. After all, *you* are the business. I'm sure there are going to be some tools and equipment you will need and will want to purchase, but it's not like you will be manufacturing goods or having to keep a stock of items to sell or anything like that." said Alexis. "You're probably right. I guess I'm also scared of falling flat on my face." said Connor. "Well, you're miserable at the police department right now, so what better time to go for it?" asked Alexis. "I might be miserable, but it's a good, steady income with benefits." replied Connor. "I have faith in you. Even if the PI business doesn't work out, I know you'll find something else. If you're miserable now, surely, you'd find something else that doesn't make you miserable." said Alexis.

Connor was the kind of person that didn't want to let go of one rung on a ladder until he had his other hand on the next one. In his mind, he could hear Alexis saying something like *If you have to juggle while you're climbing a ladder, you may not get to hold on at all.* Connor wanted to get a PI business ready to go before he handed in his resignation to the department. He had spotted a potentially perfect place for an office, still in the city, but closest to shantytown, where the rent would probably be the lowest.

Connor had arranged to meet the owner of the building over the coming weekend. He took his entire family to look at the place he had in mind. He knew it wasn't fancy, elegant, or modern, but he thought it was quite charming - and quite cheap. He was really hoping that Alexis would see the vision he had for the office. He knew Captain would like it, because *When Matey's happy, Captain's happy,* and he had a custom, hand-made t-shirt that stated as much.

Alexis did agree with Connor on the initial charm of the place. It was in Edmonton's downtown district, snuggled in between a locally-owned, authentic pizza parlor on the left and a thrift store on the right. Lavie Horowitz, was an older man who was even shorter than Connor. Connor guessed him to be in his late sixties, but his thick, dark hair seemed to have been successfully holding on to a much earlier age. He was not very talkative, but when he did, you could feel a genuine caring nature in his voice. He unlocked the glass door entrance that led directly into a short, narrow hallway. Connor proudly daydreamed and saw his name in plain, black letters on the door, with *Private Investigator* printed underneath, in place of the *Johnson Insurance* that was currently displayed on the door. Mr. Horowitz led them to the end of the hallway, where there was a door on the left and one on the right. The one on the left was plain, and the one on the right displayed the simple symbols of a man, a woman, and a wheelchair, with the word *BATHROOM* under the symbols.

Mr. Horowitz unlocked the left door, and entered, motioning for the family to follow him into the room. Save for a stand-up fan in the corner, and a very old-looking but solid desk, the room was empty. The room was small, and appeared to possibly have been created by utilizing a portion of the pizza parlor. Assuming Connor would want a couple of filing cabinets, and a few small end-tables, Alexis could easily see room enough for two chairs to face the desk, and another one in the corner. She doubted that there would ever be more people at one time to fill more than three chairs, but if it did ever come up, they would just have to use chair arms, end tables, or just stand.

"With a little cleaning, a few pieces of furniture, and a woman's touch, I can see it turning out to be very quaint." said Alexis. "Well, let's go lightly on the woman's touch, this is a manly PI office." said Connor, jokingly. "So, no pink furnishings, then?" she asked, smiling. "I like it, Dad. This is your secret mancave." said Captain, hugging his father. "Yes, it could be. I like it, too, Son." said Connor, ruffling his son's hair. "The previous tenant seemed very pleased with the space. He only left because he ended up going to work for a big-name insurance company. He said it was just too much competition between them and the fact that about everything can be done online now." said Mr. Horowitz. "I believe it. I know I will be utilizing the internet for my new career, but fortunately, there aren't robots to do the foot-work . . . *yet.*" said Connor. He had known Mr. Horowitz for a long time, and his family had met him before out and about in town. He had responded to various domestic calls at a couple of Mr. Horowitz's apartment buildings when he was a beat cop. No one ever had anything negative to say about Mr. Horowitz. He was the exception to the rule, at least as far as landlord complaints go, as far as Connor knew. Because of the nice guy he was, and the fact that Mr. Horowitz liked the Gellar family, he gave Connor a better deal than he could have ever hoped for. Not only that, he did not make him sign a lease, but agreed on a month-to-month rental on a handshake. This was definitely a relief to Connor, who was unsure of himself. He was hopeful for his PI business, but still felt a little skeptical of its success. He, of course, didn't share that feeling with anyone.

The three Gellars had spent the weekend bringing Connor's office up to Alexis' standards. There were some items that she thought needed to be bought new, but some of them were conveniently purchased from the thrift store next door to the office. Connor was grateful that Alexis loved that old desk, as it was so heavy, that it took all three of them just to move it to where Alexis thought it would be best. He had no idea how it had even had been brought in, not just due to the weight, but the size. He jokingly thought that maybe the office had been built around the large, old desk. After a good wipe-down and an application of furniture polish, the desk looked brand-new. By Sunday afternoon, the office met with the *Alexis Seal of Approval.*

| 7 |

Chapter 7: Pulling the Trigger

Monday morning, Connor had serious butterflies in his stomach. It was funny how when you are going to make a dramatic change in your life, sometimes, all you could think about were the negative things that could happen. His saving grace for his decision to leave the force was that he would be happier doing *anything* instead of desk duty. He knew remaining at the force would leave him unhappy. Even if he failed at being a PI, and had to find other employment, he would rather start fresh. He didn't want to be continually prompted with memories of the circumstances that could lead him to be in one of any number of other police administrative duties that were available to him.

Connor diligently performed his duties, processing the red tape documentation that goes along with most branches of government services. Because it was who he was, he intended

28

to continue to perform his duties to the best of his abilities, no matter how mundane he felt they were, up until his last day with the department. His stomach was already in knots when Captain Lester walked into the office, and it felt as if the knots cinched inside of him even tighter. "Good morning, Gellar." said the captain. "Good morning, Sir." responded Connor. He sensed the slight discomfort in the captain's voice. He knew that Captain Lester liked him and was not happy about Connor's circumstances either. Connor watched the captain go into his office, and then inhaled deeply. He released the air in his lungs slowly through his nose, and then stood up. He walked toward the captain's office, holding his statement of resignation in his hand.

Connor's hand was inches away from the door jamb, just about to do his courtesy knock, when the captain said "Come on in, Gellar." Connor was slightly surprised, as he knew the captain could not see him nor his hand from his place behind his desk. Connor walked into Captain Lester's office with a look of puzzlement on his face. "You can't make it through some of the things I've been through, and be where I am today without having some sort of ESP that works from time to time. You're a good man, Connor. I'd ask you to reconsider, but I know that would just make the decision you have already made that much harder to follow through with." said the captain. Connor was dumbfounded and momentarily at a loss for words. He had already somewhat played out in his head how he was going to approach his C/O and what he was going to say, but the captain's intuition threw most of it out the window. "Sir, it has been an honor working here and for you. These have been some of the best years of my life."

Connor finally managed. Captain Lester stood up and offered his hand, which Connor took. "The honor is mine as well, Connor. You made my job a lot easier and definitely more interesting. I wish you all the best." Connor handed in his resignation letter.

After he had turned in his resignation letter, he had found that the knots in his stomach had loosened a little. He was working a standard two-week notice, and he hoped that he had a chance to tell Daniel before he had found out from someone else. He knew he could always call Daniel, but that just didn't feel right. If Daniel did find out, Connor would just tell him that other than the captain, he was going to be the next to know. Captain Lester was good about keeping things private that were not necessary to share. Connor picked up a stack of papers and moved them closer to him on his desk, and began entering information from the papers into the computer. *Two more weeks.* he thought.

As it turned out, Daniel came by the department before Connor left for the day. He made his way directly to Connor's desk. Daniel's partner, Rachel, had followed him in, but she headed toward the door that led to other areas of the department. Daniel's eyes followed her to the door and said "I'll catch up with you." to her. "Ten-four." she said plainly. She didn't even acknowledge Connor. Daniel turned back toward Connor. Ripping off the bandage before Daniel could even speak, Connor said "Daniel, I've put in my resignation today. I don't know why Rachel seems to ignore and avoid me; the circumstances are just what they are. I thought I put her at ease by talking to her before." Daniel was slightly taken back from Connor's news. His facial expression gave Connor the impression that he had other things on his mind, but now he seemed to hold back. "No way! Man, I don't want to see you go!" exclaimed Daniel. "There's nothing for me here, anymore, Daniel. I'm not happy doing this desk job, and I won't be happy doing anything else they have to offer here." said Connor. "What're you going to do?" asked Daniel. "Well, Edmonton isn't a huge city, but based upon my research, it's big enough to give a decent living to a private investigator. You know how many cases we've reluctantly had to close. There is definitely a demand for someone that can privately get to the bottom of some of these cases and find out more information than our superiors give us leeway to do." said Connor. Daniel nodded his head slowly; his eyes had slightly glazed over in deep thought. "You won't get any argument there." Daniel said, softly. Connor could see the disappointment in his glazed eyes, but he could also sense that something else seemed to be troubling his old partner. Connor was just about to ask Daniel if everything was okay, when Daniel seemed to snap out of his mental preoccupation. "So, we need to get a big party lined up for you, buddy!" exclaimed Daniel. Connor raised both of his hands as if to hold Daniel at bay and shook his head slowly. "No way, Daniel. You know me well enough not to do that." he said, seriously. Daniel did indeed know that his buddy was not a big fan of social gatherings, especially if he would be the primary focus. "Promise me you won't." Connor added, earnestly. "Okay, okay. You'll at least let *me* take you out for lunch one day, right?" asked Daniel. "Of course, buddy, thanks." said Connor. "Well, I guess congratulations are in order, then. I'll give you a call one day before your last day, and we'll grab lunch, *Mr. Big Shot PI.*" said Daniel. Connor chuckled. Daniel affectionately clapped Connor on the back and then headed to the door that Rachel had entered a few minutes before.

| **8** |

Chapter 8: I've Got Friends in No Places

Only that call never came. In fact, Connor had not seen Daniel again since he had told him of his resignation, a full two weeks ago. Today was his last day with the department. He pulled out his cellphone and looked at it blankly. No texts. No missed calls. It was almost 11:00am, and Daniel knew that Connor liked to eat lunch around 11:30am. *Should I call him?* Connor thought. He replaced his phone in its holster and walked over to Captain Lester's office, and knocked on the door jamb. "Come in." said the captain. "Hi, Captain Lester." said Connor. "Short timer! It's your last day, partner." exclaimed the captain. "Yes Sir. Have you seen Daniel around?" Connor asked the captain. "I saw him at our meeting just this morning." said Captain Lester. "Hmm. Did he seem to be acting okay to you?" asked Connor. "Well, honestly, I have noticed that he's not his usual, chipper self. I believe that between the shooting incident, breaking in a new partner, and you leaving the department, he has been overwhelmed. Who knows, he may also have other worries on his mind as well." said Captain Lester. "Well, yeah, I can understand that. It's just that he had said he wanted to take me out for lunch before I left, and I haven't even seen him since the day I told him I was leaving. That was the same day I turned in my resignation, two weeks ago." said Connor. The captain pursed his lips and lowered his eyebrows. "I know you have had a bad break, Connor, so no disrespect concerning your leg, but all of the changes may have been just as hard on him as they were on you . . ." said Captain Lester. "Try giving him a call." the captain added. Connor nodded and said "I will. Thanks, Captain." He returned to his desk.

Connor sat back down at his desk and pulled out his cellphone. He stared at it for several minutes, thinking. He was hesitant to call. Connor believed that there was no way Daniel would have forgotten about him. This could only mean one thing, which is that Daniel had been intentionally avoiding him. Even if Captain Lester was right about the situation also being very mentally hard on Daniel, Connor just couldn't accept that his partner and friend would part ways like this. Reluctantly, Connor dialed the contact number for Daniel's cellphone. His trepidation was realized when after the fourth ring, Daniel's voicemail message began to play. Connor's mind raced for what he was going to say when leaving a voicemail. When Daniel's voicemail message finished playing and the phone beeped, Connor opened his mouth to speak. Thinking twice, he closed his mouth and pressed the end button on his cellphone. He had a mixture of emotions pouring through him. Was his friend so hurt that he couldn't even face him? Was his friend secretly jealous of the move he was making? Was his friend so involved with his new partner that he no longer cared about him? Did his friend ever really care about him? Connor wasn't sure whether he should feel concerned, apathetic, or angry. Not having known what day Daniel had been planning on calling him for lunch, he had still brought his lunch every day. He began eating his lunch quietly, while he continued working on the reports at his desk. He kept a check on his phone and looked every time he heard a door open. Deep down, he hoped that Daniel would call or come in with an apology and some sort of legitimate excuse for his seemingly dismissive behavior. When quitting time finally came, he gathered the few remaining personal items he had at the department, said a final farewell to Captain Lester, and then left the building.

| 9 |

Chapter 9: Gellar Investigative Services

Connor and Alexis both had previously thought of the many ways they could advertise Connor's new business, such as social media, the local papers, local TV spots, etc. He had started his PI business the Monday after leaving the department. That weekend, he had his new PI business logo up on his door. By the time lunchtime had rolled around, Connor already had five prospective clients come in to his office, with two of them actually hiring him. Unsurprisingly, four out of the five prospects were for infidelity and one of them was for insurance fraud. He ended up being hired by a woman that suspected her husband of cheating, and an insurance company that was paying a disability claim and expected that their claimant was lying to them about their abilities. The other three prospective clients were interested, but Connor believed that sticker shock scared them away. Even though he was the first and only PI in their city, he still tried to price his services at fair, competitive prices, but these services weren't cheap when all the time and expenses were considered.

Connor began working his first case for Mrs. Ericson, the one with the suspected cheater, the following morning. Connor already had a DSLR, as photography was one of his hobbies. He did purchase an expensive zoom lens, however, as he knew he would eventually need it on other cases. He was not into flashy automobiles, so his plain, silver sedan was the perfect stakeout vehicle. He tailed the suspect as the man headed to work. The man went straight to work, uneventfully. Connor parked on the street, just outside of the employee parking area. He brought snacks and water to keep his metabolism going throughout the day. He brought a newspaper to help alleviate the boredom the drawn-out waiting would bring upon him. He also brought a portable urinal, an absolute necessity for lengthy stakeouts.

As he was reading the newspaper, Connor's peripheral vision picked up some movement. Sure enough, it was the suspect, and he was leaving work two hours earlier than his wife had told him of the man's schedule. Connor allowed the man to make some distance before he pulled out and followed him. Having been a police detective for so long, he was an expert at tailing a suspect without getting noticed. He followed the man to *Fresh Breeze Park*, a local park that Connor knew to be a popular meeting place. There was one particular area in the park that offered decent concealment and privacy to a vehicle. He had even been there himself, as a younger man. He knew that he was on to something when another car pulled up beside the suspect's car. Connor was parked far enough away so as to not arouse any suspicion, but his new, high-powered, lens zoomed in enough to clearly see the face of the woman getting into the suspect's car. Connor snapped several pictures of the woman as she entered his car, and of the two vehicles sitting together, including their license plates. He watched the two people through his camera's viewfinder and would snap a photo whenever a particularly good shot of their faces would show. After a few minutes, the mystery woman and the man had disappeared from Connor's view of them through the man's windshield.

He got out of his car and using his stealth training, quietly and discretely found a better vantage point in which to photograph the two lovers. As he had figured, they were both prone in the seat. Considering the throes of passion they were currently in, he doubted that they would have noticed him anyway. After satisfactorily obtaining the shots he wanted, Connor slipped back into his vehicle. He waited patiently until the woman got out of the suspect's car. He snapped a few more photos of her for good measure, in case any of the others he had taken turned out to be blurry. Fortunately, the suspect pulled away first, perhaps worried about getting home on time. Once his female rendezvous had pulled away, Connor tailed her. She went to a nearby grocery store. *Good grief, I bet if she's also married, she's going to use the supermarket as her alibi.* Connor thought. Fortunately, she wasn't in the store as long as one might have expected, and then she was on the road again. This time, she apparently went to her house, as she used a garage door opener to access the garage. He, of course, would verify all identities and pertinent information before he prepared a report package for his client.

Using the resources available to him as a PI, Connor was able to identify the female that the man had met. As Connor had suspected from the trip to the supermarket, she was also married. When his client came to him, he had a complete package prepared for her. The package contained items such as the report, any media obtained, and the bill. The report contained items such as a report number, the date (subsequent surveillance will not be required in this particular case), the times of the suspect's movements, the mystery woman's information, and a narrative of the events that took place. The media provided in this case were the pictures that he had printed on his professional printer. He did not want to give unnecessary access to a client's private business, by having pictures printed somewhere. She had already given him his retainer fee, and the bill contained the balance, including the expenses he had incurred. He was proud of the work he had done, but he gained no satisfaction from confirming his client's suspicions. Mrs. Ericson seemed to have a mixture of emotions. Her eyes showed relief from the fact that there was now no doubt that she had a cheating husband, and the tears that fell from them portrayed the broken heart and betrayal she was experiencing. She paid Connor the remainder of the bill in cash, and he hand-wrote her a receipt from a receipt booklet he had picked up from an office store. She placed the receipt, along with the other items from the package back into the folder that Connor had provided. He verbally consoled the woman the best he could, but he had learned a long time ago not to have physical contact in situations such as these.

During his stakeout the day before, Connor had to let all of his calls go to voicemail. Many of the voicemails that he had received were inquiries about hiring him. After having met with Mrs. Ericson, he had even more people coming in to inquire about hiring him. Several of the calls he returned resulted in people scheduling times to meet with him to discuss their needs. Several of the walk-ins had hired him. Business was good. But he was only one man, so he could only do so much. As it stood, unless there was a pressing issue, by which Connor would eventually figure out how he could charge for it, he intended on working the cases in the order in which they came in to him. He was also going to have to figure out a schedule in which some days would be field days, and some would be meeting with clients and prospective clients. He currently had placed a flip sign on his door that read ***On assignment. Please call and leave a message.*** with his phone number at the bottom.

The days flew by. Connor had never been happier. He was living his childhood dream *and* he was his own boss. Because of who he is, Connor never stopped learning. He was constantly absorbing classes and training as his schedule would allow. He would be well ahead of the required credit hours for maintaining a PI license by the time the two-year renewal rolled around. Over the course of months, Connor's business had become reputable and well-established in the community. Although, he had made many people angry, as well, by having their misdeeds uncovered. On top of the many tips and tricks he had learned from training and additional research, as he could afford to, he had also picked up various gadgets that would prove to be useful for various scenarios in future cases. He still had fond memories of his coworkers and the police department and had cause to interact with them on several occasions for different reasons relating to different cases. He would think of Daniel from time to time and wonder what and how he was doing. He wasn't about to call him. Maybe it was pride. As it was now, Daniel still held a small place in his heart as an old friend. If he did call him and he didn't answer *again,* Connor didn't think he would have any feelings left for him at all.

| 10 |

Chapter 10: Something Did Seem too Good to be True

Captain was waiting at the side door connected to the garage when Connor walked in. "Matey!" exclaimed Captain. "Hey, my wonderful Captain!" exclaimed Connor. They embraced and held each other for several moments. "Mommy don't feel good." Captain volunteered. "She doesn't? What's wrong with Mom?" asked Connor. "She's sick, Daddy." said Captain, solemnly. Most of the house lights were off, which was unusual. In an effort to conserve energy, Connor usually stayed on them both to keep lights turned off except for in the rooms that they were using. Connor followed Captain to the master bedroom. Alexis was lying on the bed, fully dressed, except for her shoes. Her eyes had been closed, but she opened them when Captain and Connor entered the room. "Hey, babe . . . what's wrong?" Connor asked. Captain had laid on the bed beside his mom and laid his head on her shoulder. He stroked her hair and she stroked his. "I just got to feeling really tired and my stomach hurts. I'm sorry." Alexis said. "Honey, you don't need to be sorry for not feeling good." said Connor as he kissed her on the cheek and then felt her forehead. "There's a lot of junk going around right now, I may have picked up a bug." she said. "You don't have a fever, but you do look a little pale. Why don't you just rest, and I'll take care of dinner tonight." said Connor. She nodded and said, "Just do something for you guys, I don't even feel like eating."

Captain helped Connor prepare their meal. They made their homemade and locally famous *Captain's Carolina Crab Cakes* with grits on the side. Basically, they were just variations of the recipes for Charleston or Maryland crab cakes, using whatever ingredients they had available, with their main ingredient being love, of course. They both ate in the office, so Alexis could rest. After eating, they played some computer games all the way up until bedtime. After seeing Captain off to bed, he went into their bedroom where Alexis was gently snoring. He quietly showered and managed to get into bed without waking her. The next morning, Alexis looked and felt a lot better. She insisted that she was well enough to go to work, so Connor helped her get Captain ready, and they all headed off to their respective destinations. Alexis and Captain, to the university, and Connor to his office.

Connor had worked out his system of scheduling for his office, and he found that what seemed to work best for him was to be in the office on Mondays and Tuesdays, as that was when most of his prospective clients came in. He would do most of his investigations on Thursdays, Fridays, and weekends when necessary. He left Wednesdays open to going either way, if he needed more office time, or needed to start an investigation sooner. It wasn't perfect, but it was working pretty well. The advertisements had been a really big help in the beginning, but he was pleasantly surprised when he discovered how many people had been sent to him by word-of-mouth recommendations.

More months had passed, and Connor's success had continued to increase. He giddily thought that he was getting to the point where he was either going to have to explain to potential clients that there was going to be a very long wait, simply turn them away, or he was going to have to consider getting some help. His happy life seemed too good to be true.

Too good to be true it was. It was past 4:00 pm when he received a call from the university while he was in the middle of speaking to a prospective client. "Oh my! Where's Captain?" Connor asked, tensely. After a brief pause, he exclaimed "I'm on my way there!" He hung up the phone. His prospective client was looking at him with concern. "I'm very sorry, but I've got to go, it's a family emergency." said Connor. The man stood up and said "Certainly. I hope everything turns out okay." Connor said "Thank you. I'll call you just as soon as I am able to." The prospective client nodded, and they both hurried out of the office, with Connor locking up as he left. He jumped in his sedan and hurried to the hospital that was closest to the university where Alexis worked.

When he arrived, he rushed into the emergency room and gave the nurse at the station Alexis' name. "She's with a doctor now. Your family is in the waiting room." said the nurse. She pointed the way, and Connor took off. He spotted Captain sitting next to one of Alexis' good friends and coworkers, Francis. He could remember her, as she and her husband had been to the house a few times for dinner. He rushed to them. Captain looked scared and Connor could tell he had been crying. Captain stood and Connor hugged him and stroked his hair. "It's going to be okay, buddy." Connor said to his son. He looked over at Francis. "Do you know what happened?" he asked. "I am just passing on what I have heard from the students. She was in the middle of a lecture, and she just collapsed. One of her students ran across the hall and got me. I checked her. She had a pulse and was breathing, but unresponsive, so I called 911. The ambulance came and got her, and I took Captain and drove us here to the hospital." Francis was starting to tear up. Connor extended his arm to include her in the hug he was sharing with his son. She joined them.

After their embrace, Connor went to the closest nurse's station to inquire about his wife. She explained to Connor that the doctor was still with her right now, and she would let Connor know as soon as the doctor was ready to talk to him. Connor exhaled and returned to the waiting area with Captain and Francis. After several hours of waiting, a doctor finally did come out to talk to Connor. "Mr. Gellar?" the doctor asked, in a strong Hindi accent. "I am Dr. Burman. Your wife has regained consciousness, but she is very weak. We are running quite a few tests to try and figure out what has happened. I will allow you to see her, but please keep it brief. Let her know you are here and we are doing everything we can to find out what is wrong. ICU Room 607." he finished. Connor Nodded and said, "Thank you, Doctor."

Connor quietly walked into the room. "Honey?" he said in a whisper. Alexis opened her eyes and offered the bravest smile she could muster. Connor could see she was getting ready to speak. "Don't speak. The doctor said you are still very weak. They are running tests on you now, trying to figure out what happened and what is wrong. Captain is in the waiting room with Francis." He approached the hospital bed and kissed her on the cheek, while he reached for her hand and gripped it. "The doctor said it would be best to keep my visit brief. I just wanted you to know we are here, we love you, and we're going to do everything we can to get you better." Connor could feel her squeeze his hand gently and she smiled once again. He kissed her once more on the cheek and said "Whatever it is, we'll get through it." One of the nurses came in, pushing a cart loaded with various medical items. He stroked Alexis' hair, then walked out of the room.

"Francis, she's going to be here all night." Connor said, looking at Captain who was sleeping in a chair. "I've got that sweet, young man. I know all about his needs, thanks to Alexis. He can come with me to work tomorrow, just like he does with his mom." said Francis. Relief washed over Connor's face. He didn't want Captain to have to sleep in the hospital. He hugged Francis and said, "Thank you." Connor walked over to Captain and gently shook his shoulder. Captain opened his eyes. "Mommy is going to spend the night in the hospital and Daddy is going to stay with her. You're going to go spend the night with Francis and David, and she's going to take you to the university with her tomorrow, okay?" asked

Connor. Captain yawned and nodded. "Tell Mommy I love her." said Captain. "I will, buddy. I love you, and don't worry about Mommy, she's going to be okay." said Connor. Captain nodded. Connor gave him a hug and kiss, then Francis locked arms with Captain, and they headed down the hallway.

As worried as he was, Connor still managed to sleep in the waiting room. He had been burning the candle at both ends, and he was physically and mentally exhausted. He woke the following morning to Dr. Burman gently shaking him. "Mr. Gellar?" said the doctor. Connor opened his eyes. Realizing where he was, Connor jumped up. "Dr. Burman, how is Alexis?" Connor asked, anxiously. "She is stable, Mr .Gellar, but I need to talk to you in private. Please follow me." said Dr. Burman. Connor's stomach knotted up. He knew something was wrong, otherwise, he would have just talked to him in the waiting room. He followed the doctor to an office, where Dr. Burman sat behind a desk, and offered Connor to take the chair in front of him. "Mr. Gellar, I'm sorry to have to be the bearer of bad news." began Dr. Burman. Connor's stomach did flip-flops. "Your wife has pancreatic cancer." he continued. The doctor paused to let Connor process what he had just said. It was a good thing because he probably wouldn't have heard anything directly after that nasty c-word. Finally, after a few moments of contemplating the words that just came out of the doctor's mouth, Connor asked "How bad is it?" Dr. Burman looked down and then back at Connor. "I'm afraid it's very bad. I really can't believe that she has made it this long without any other symptoms. However, a long duration of asymptomatic pancreatic cancer going from stage to stage can also be quite common." said the doctor. Connor felt nauseous. He again took a little time to gather his thoughts in the middle of feeling as if his entire life was falling apart. "What can we do?" Connor asked, holding on to hope. The doctor again broke eye contact with Connor before he spoke. "There's really nothing we can do, except make her as comfortable as possible in the time that she has left." said Dr. Burman. That was the final gut punch that nearly took Connor out. "There's nothing you can do?" Connor almost shouted the question. "Mr. Gellar, pancreatic cancer can be very aggressive. She has had it a while now, with no symptoms before the past few days. It is very common that a person reaches stage IV before it gets detected. The cancer has already metastasized well beyond the pancreas. Any treatment we could provide would not only be ineffective but would most likely increase her suffering in the short time she has left." said the doctor, solemnly. Connor sat silently for several minutes. He knew the doctor had a busy schedule, and yet afforded him the respect of patience for what he was going through. "Does she know?" Connor asked, more quietly this time. "Yes, I told her this morning. She has already expressed she does not want treatment." said Dr. Burman. Connor placed his hand on his forehead and then asked, "How long do you think she has?" Connor could see in Dr. Burman's eyes that he was not going to like the answer. "There are many factors that make disease progression different for every individual. Typically, some-one in your wife's condition may only have months." said Dr. Burman as he stood up and walked around his desk to where Connor sat. "I'm very sorry, Mr. Gellar." he added, placing a hand on Connor's shoulder.

Connor walked into his wife's hospital room. He tried to be strong, but he had tears in his eyes. Alexis was awake and reached her arms out to him. He laid his upper body on his wife and squeezed as hard as he dared. "It's going to be okay, baby." she said to him. "Let's go home. I want to be home." she said.

Connor made all of the arrangements to get his wife moved home. He learned every step he needed to do in order to take care of her. He learned every medicine she needed to take to keep her as healthy and as pain-free as possible.

Chapter 11: My Angel

Connor cared for his wife, and kept her as comfortable as possible. He did absolutely everything for her. He didn't have the heart to explain to Captain that his mother was dying. On one occasion, Alexis had told Connor that she was so glad it was her and not him. "I would trade places with you if I could, honey." he told her. "I know you would. Connor. I also know that Captain loves me. But he wouldn't make it without you. You are his hero. You are his world." Alexis said. Connor was momentarily silent. "But *you* are his *Angel.*" said Connor, referring to the endearing term Captain had given his mother years ago. "And I always will be." she said, smiling in spite of her pain. Connor returned her smile.

Both of Alexis' parents had died years ago. It was cruel sarcasm that both of them had succumbed to cancer. Connor was still fortunate enough to have both of his parents, but they were both elderly and just getting by not only physically, but financially as well, on their fixed incomes. Neither Connor nor Alexis had any extended family that could help them. There were a few friends that they might could count on, but Connor could not get himself to put them in such a difficult position.

He told Mr. Horowitz that he could no longer rent the office anymore due to his circumstances. Mr. Horowitz told Connor he would hold off renting the office for as long as he could. Connor called all of his clients with current cases and apologized for having to back out of the work. He simply told them the truth and they all seemed sympathetic to his situation. He lied to Alexis and told her that he had a part-time job working online, and that's how he was paying the bills. When, in actuality, all of their small retirement funds were gone, all of their meager savings were completely depleted, and Connor had borrowed as much as the bank would let him against their home. When he was not in the room with her, he would tell her he was checking in on his job. In reality, oftentimes, he was crying in private.

Indeed, several months had passed before it happened. The night was calm and the stars were bright. Connor was roused by his wife's voice as she spoke, late in the hour. "Connor?" Alexis had asked a few times in her weak voice in order to wake her husband. He sat up in bed, switched on the bedside lamp, and turned to his wife. She had always been and still was beautiful, but under the lamplight, Connor could really see how she had really diminished in size, was very pale and jaundiced. "Yes, Dear. Are you okay? Can I get you something?" he asked in a whisper. She was quiet for a moment. "It's time, honey." she said weakly. "Time? Time for what?" he asked, slightly confused. "It's *my* time, honey. Go get Captain." she said. "No, baby, no. You probably just need some medicine . . ." Connor began. Alexis reached out to him and gripped his hand, interrupting him. "Connor, I can *feel* it. I'm barely holding on. Get Captain, because I want to talk to you both before I go. Hurry." she said weakly. Connor's eyes began spilling tears. He released her hand and hurried out of their bedroom. He came back with his scared and disoriented son. They both climbed into the bed next to Alexis. "Hey, baby." Alexis said weakly to Captain, as she stroked the hair on his head. "Hey, Mommy." said Captain. "Listen, baby. Mommy has to go, now. I want you to stay strong and always be happy. I want you to always know that Mommy loves you and I will be watching over you." said Alexis. "Mommy, go where?" Captain asked. "Baby, Mommy has to go to heaven." she said. "No, Mommy, don't go to heaven, now." said Captain, softly, as he placed his hand on the side of her face. Connor's eyes were streaming, but he struggled to hold onto his composure, so as not to upset Captain further. Alexis pulled Captain in and hugged him around his neck. "Jesus needs me there, my sweet man. He wants me to be an angel." she said. "Mommy, you are *my* angel." Captain said as he began to cry. Connor joined their embrace, turning it into a three-way hug, no longer able to hold back the vocalizations of his anguish.

Memories flashed back in Connor's mind to one of their first three-way hugs. Captain was about two years old. Connor and Alexis had been arguing about something. In the heat of the moment, they had not noticed that Captain had been watching them. They could see he was on the verge of tears from watching his parents yell at each other. Connor had scooped him up and walked over to Alexis, so they both could comfort and assure him. Once he was close to Alexis, Captain had reached his arms out, one toward Connor's head and the other toward Alexis' head. At first, they both thought it was just to perform a three-way hug. As they tightened up their circle, so Captain could reach them, he proceeded to push their heads together. They realized that Captain was forcing their faces toward each other for a kiss! Connor and Alexis kissed. This was followed by Captain's little arms going around his parents' necks and pulling them in for the three-way hug.

Alexis loosened her grip on the two men, who pulled away and gave her some breathing room. She forced herself to stop crying and wiped the tears from her eyes. "Listen, my two men." began Alexis, as she gripped one of each man's hands with one of her own. Both Connor and Captain had also stopped crying, but they were both still sniffling as their tears had begun to ease up. "My two men. I love you both so much. My life with you two has been the happiest that any woman could ever hope for. I don't regret anything. I don't know how anyone could have had a fuller, more interesting life, than the one I have shared with my guys. You two deserve to live the rest of your lives as happy as I have lived mine. But you are both wonderful messes. You have to take care of each other now and live the happiest lives you can. Will you two promise me that?" Alexis finished, nearly out of breath. Both men nodded. "I love you, honey. I only wish there was more time to show you just how much." said Connor, as new tears began to roll down his cheeks. "You have already shown me." she said smiling and nodding in the direction of Captain, as she lovingly turned her gaze to her son. "I love you, Mommy! You will always be my angel!" Captain exclaimed, as he started to cry again and moved in closer to hug his mother tightly. Connor also moved in closer for the last three-way hug with his family. "Yes, baby, I will always be your angel." whispered Alexis. And then she was gone.

| 12 |

Chapter 12: Shambles

The Gellars were Christians, only it had been a while since they had been members of any certain church. There was, however, one church in particular that they had attended more frequently than any other. This was a church where they had enjoyed some services and special times alongside some of their closest friends. When these friends had heard of Alexis' passing, they took it upon themselves to speak to the pastor about presiding over her service. Being the kind-hearted pastor she was, as all pastors should be, there was no hesitation in her acceptance of being the officiant if that was Connor's desire. Connor was very grateful for his friends' intercession, otherwise, the service would have been completely performed at the funeral home. Not that there was necessarily anything wrong with that, but Connor felt that it would have been more pleasing to Alexis to be at a church that held some precious memories. Connor was not up to doing a visitation. The house was upside-down from where he had let it go during Alexis' illness. He was sad, and depressed, and had no energy to prepare it for guests. He knew without a doubt that someone would have stepped in, be he wasn't about to impose on anyone else.

Although Connor did not feel as if they had a lot of friends, he was surprised at the large turnout for her funeral. Some of the attendees even had to stand in the back of the church. Pastor Swanson performed a beautiful service. She was very eloquent and yet did not stray from her Christian beliefs in the delivery of her message of hope near the end of the service. Connor had said to many people, Christian believers and non-believers alike, that if he and Alexis' had not done anything right in this life, they did the one thing that counted, and that was to have their son believe in Jesus. Alexis had made sure that Captain was always able to attend the one, particular private Christian school in the area, that had absolutely no reservations to accommodate Captain with whatever needs he had. It had been a little shameful at some of the excuses and responses that other schools, including Christian schools, had come up with for not being able to make adaptations to Captain's minor needs. The principal at the school had said *He's a child of God like any other and we will do everything we can to see to it that he gets all the help we can give him.* Connor had never really lived the Christian life as he believed he should live it, but that principal was probably responsible for Connor not losing his faith altogether. Not only had it been a wonderful experience for Captain, but Connor also felt that it was a wonderful experience for the rest of the typical school-children that attended as well. Not only did the students there get a solid, practical education, but they also got immersed in the teachings of the Christian religion. Captain let the other children get a first-hand lesson on being humble and having humility. He only had to be his unique, loving self to show the students that although we are all different, we are also all the same in the eyes of God.

Word had evidently gotten around, as Connor was not much on broadcasting events that happened in his life, even in cases such as these. Connor's parents were there, but he did have to make arrangements for their transportation. There were quite a few of their mutual friends among the attendees. There were some of Alexis' coworkers, and Connor knew a few of them, including Francis and her husband, David. Captain Lester and several of the officers Connor had worked with over the years had come. Connor quickly noticed that Daniel was not among them. Some of Captain's old friends from school and their parents had come. There were even some of Connor's clients that he had helped with particularly sticky situations that were among the attendees. It gave Connor a good feeling to know that there were quite a few people who either cared about Alexis, Captain, or himself enough to come to the service.

Initially, when they had talked about death, Alexis had wanted to be cremated. She had always said that she wanted her ashes to be spread in the ocean, as the beach was her favorite place in the world. Ultimately, however, she had decided she would rather be placed in one of her family's plots to be near her mother and father. Whether one has religion or not, Connor always believed it to be a comforting thought for your final resting place to be near a loved one. Connor honored her wishes.

It was a very sunny day, but the gentle breeze kept it from being uncomfortable, as Pastor Swanson delivered her final message over Alexis in the Divine Rest cemetery in Edmonton. Some of their friends were crying, and Connor's mother was crying, but it was Captain's tender heart that seemed to pronounce the greatest grief. Connor kept his arm over Captain's shoulders, doing his best to ease his pain. Between Connor trying to keep it together and be strong for his son to lean on, and the fact that he had already cried out so many tears, he managed to maintain composure. After the final words, some of the attendees left, while some formed a line to pay more personal respects to Connor and Captain. He appreciated everyone, but Connor knew he wouldn't remember much about who said what. He gave the obligatory nod, a word of thanks, and a handshake or hug, however, the person had led him. Captain, being more of a social butterfly like his mother, had a few words and a hug for everyone. Connor felt guilty, as much as he loved Alexis, he just wanted this day to be over.

It seemed like forever, but the crowd finally began dispersing. Captain led Connor over to the various flower arrangements surrounding his mother's casket. He looked at them, and then back at his dad, without saying a word. There were a few occasions that Connor, along with others, which included Alexis, could not always understand everything that Captain was trying to say the first time he said it. Oftentimes, you had to be patient and persistent to finally understand the message he was trying to convey. But Connor also felt that he and his son had a very special bond. One could call it paternal instinct, but at times, Connor had joked with others about how he felt as if they had some form of special father-son telepathy. In this instance, he knew exactly what Captain was asking him. "You can take whatever flowers you want, son. Mommy would like that." said Connor. Captain went to the arrangement that was from him and his dad and pulled one of the yellow roses off of it. This was his mother's favorite flower. Connor also pulled a yellow rose off and laid it on top of Alexis' casket. Connor thanked the few remaining people, and then he and his son began walking to their car, side-by-side with their arms on each other's shoulders. Connor had elected not to ride in the limo but drove in the procession as everyone else. He had plans to send something special to Pastor Swanson, but he would have to do it later. As he approached his sedan, he and Captain removed their arms from each other's shoulders. Captain got into the passenger side of the car. Connor looked back at the graveside tent and around the cemetery as he exhaled. "Goodbye my love." he said. He opened the car door. Before he entered the car, he had noticed another sedan several roads away in the cemetery. It was pulling away and headed out the cemetery gate. Connor could swear it had been Daniel's car. He got in and buckled his seat belt, while verifying that Captain had buckled his own. Connor loosened his tie and put his car into drive. They headed home.

Captain slept with Connor that night, which eventually became the norm. Connor didn't mind, as he knew that they both missed Alexis. They had both slept terribly that night, and Connor often heard Captain whimpering in his sleep, that is after sleep had finally found him. They both slept late the following morning, which was another habit that formed with Alexis absent. Connor had slipped into a deep depression and was managing to keep it together just enough to take care of Captain.

Fortunately, Alexis had a small insurance policy, but that had just barely covered the expenses associated with her funeral. Connor searched and found their box of multi-occasional cards, and filled one out for Pastor Swanson. He included a $100, thanked her, and told her that the service had been beautiful. He called the lien holders for their home and automobiles and had been granted three-month extensions for all, in light of the circumstances. He figured he may eventually try to sell Alexis' car. Although he did take care of his son, by making sure he was fed, bathed, and had brushed his teeth, that was all either of them was really doing. No haircuts. No nail trimmings. No time out in the community. All of their necessities were delivered. Connor ignored most phone calls. The funds he had previously borrowed were getting dangerously low. Over the course of several weeks, they basically had turned into a father-son hermit team.

One day, out of the blue, there was a knock on the door. Connor had been sleeping, and it startled him awake. He jumped up and ran to the window beside the door and pulled the curtain back just far enough to see out. It was Alexis' co-worker, Francis. She had seen the curtain move. *Drats! Now she knows I'm here.* Connor thought. She knocked again, this time saying "Connor, I know you're there." After her being there for them at the hospital that night, he couldn't ignore her. He rushed to the bedroom and threw some clothes on and then rushed back to the front door and started unlocking it. *My hair, I forgot to comb my hair.* Connor thought, but it was too late, as she had already heard him beginning to open the door. He opened the inner door, but did not open the storm door or invite her in. "Hi, Francis. How're you?" Connor asked. "I'm more concerned with how you two are." she replied. Connor didn't know what to say. "Are you going to ask me in?" she asked. "Oh, yeah, absolutely. Sorry, where are my manners?" he asked, rhetorically. He pushed the storm door open and Francis entered their home.

Francis Herndon was a good ten years senior to Connor. She was a little shorter than the average woman, with a headful of thick, tight curls, that had streaks of gray in them. She had a pleasant face, but the many wrinkles around her eyes seemed to be a tell-tale indicator that those eyes had seen a lot. Not to mention the stories that she had told during her few visits to their home. She had taught all over the United States, as she traveled with her husband who would be stationed for several years at a time. Although she had said that she loved all of her students, she was glad to finally be retired in North Carolina, where she continued to teach at the university because she loved it. She gave Connor a hug. "So, how are you doing, Connor? Where's Captain?" she asked. "I'm hanging in there, Francis. He's around here some-where, probably in the office or his mancave." said Connor. Francis looked around, somewhat awkwardly, as she and Connor stood in their front foyer. After a few more awkward moments, Connor said "Oh, please come on in and have a seat." and led her to the living room.

Connor offered Francis a seat on the couch, and he sat in the recliner. He pressed the power button that slowly extended the footrest. They sat quietly for several minutes before Connor finally broke the silence. "So, can, I get you something to eat or drink?" he asked. "Actually, I would like bottled water, if you don't mind." Francis replied. "Not at all." he said. He pressed the button to start the slow retraction of the footrest. Francis stood up and held up her hand. "Don't get up. If you don't mind, I'll get one, I remember where you keep them." said Francis, as she headed out of the living room, not giving Connor a chance to respond.

Francis could not believe her eyes. On her way to the kitchen, she saw small, random piles of dirty laundry. There were a few baskets of clean laundry placed around as well. Once she entered the kitchen, she saw both sides of the sink full of dirty dishes. There were dirty dishes in various places on the kitchen counters as well. Curiously, she quickly pulled open their dishwasher. It was full but just needed to be unloaded. *At least those were clean.* she thought. There was also a copious amount of food packages that dotted the counters. Some of them appeared to be empty. The trashcan was so full, that the lid was almost vertical. There were a few empty paper and dry good packages lying at the base of the trashcan. Francis remembered which cabinet Alexis had retrieved the bottled water from on her previous visit. When she opened the cabinet, she saw only a single bottled water sitting there. She reached in to get the bottle and then decided not to. She closed the cabinet and then walked over to the refrigerator. There was not a whole lot in the refrigerator either, to say nothing of a bottled water. She returned to the living room empty-handed.

Connor could see the disappointment on her face when she came back into the room. "Sorry about the mess in there, I've not really felt the best for the past few days." he said. Francis didn't respond. Neither Francis nor Connor spoke for several moments. "Was there not any water? Is there something else I can get you?" asked Connor. "Can I see Captain?" asked Francis. "Sure, he'd love to see you." said Connor. Although Francis had only been to their home a few times, she and Captain were probably used to seeing each other about every day at the university, with Alexis. He had heard his son speak fondly of Francis on several occasions. Connor skipped powering the footrest back to the inclined position and jumped out of the recliner. He led Francis to Captain's mancave, where he had heard the sounds of a particular game that he knew they only had on one of his game consoles.

At any given time, Captain's mancave might be somewhat in disarray. Today, however, it was completely upside-down, and it appeared that a tornado had been through it. Although Captain was not keen on keeping his play areas spotless by any stretch of the imagination, the Gellar's had always at least made him keep some kind of order and a certain level of cleanliness in those areas. Much like the kitchen, the trashcan was overflowing, with a few items spilled around the base. There were several soda cans placed around the room. There were untidy stacks of opened keep cases with the CD games and movies simply lying about, around them. Captain was sitting in his game chair, in deep concentration on whatever game he was playing. When Connor entered the room, Captain glanced from the screen and said "Matey." to acknowledge Connor's presence, and then returned his view to the game he was interacting with. "Hey, Captain. Look who's here to see you." said Connor as he stepped further into the room, making space for Francis. Captain looked up. "Francis!" he exclaimed. He paused his game and stood up and rushed to give her a hug. "Hey, Captain! How're you doing, my buddy?" asked Francis. "Good." he said, squeezing her tight. Unless he was actually doing really, really bad, "good" was usually the answer you got. Connor believed it to be an answer he gave more out of empathy than of giving a person cause for concern about his own well-being. After their embrace, Francis backed away slightly, and gave him a once-over. She had smelled his cleanliness from their embrace. He looked very healthy. Other than his clothes being mismatched, needing some basic grooming, such as a shave, a haircut, and a manicure, he seemed physically fine. "I miss you at school." said Francis. "I miss you, too. And I miss Mommy." he said, losing the smile he had been wearing. "I know you do, Sweetie." said Francis, as she gave him another hug.

Captain began to cry, and Francis held on to him. Connor placed his hand on Captain's head and rubbed it. Francis and Connor soothed him the best they could. Connor thought back to when Alexis had lost her parents. It had been a tough time for Alexis, of course, but Captain had seemed to take it worse than she did. Multiply the hurt you already feel by 100 when you see a tender-hearted, special needs adult-child grieving. Then multiply it by another 100, when that adult-child is your own. Connor, who was hurting and emotionally lost himself, also had the task of finding balance for his son. He would never curtail his son's grieving process, but from past experiences, he did not want him to continuously dwell on his loss, either. Connor wanted him to always remember his mother and the good times they had. He hated that old adage *Time Heals all Wounds.* Time may soften your pained heart, but it sure as heck doesn't heal it. He hoped that time would soon begin to ease Captain's pain, along with his own. For right now, that's all he could hope for. Well, that, and a little misdirection. As Captain's tears began to ease up, Connor said "Hey, Captain. I wonder if Francis has seen your new game?" Captain released Francis and looked at her through his tear-swollen eyes. Connor, with that father-son telepathy, could see in his face and actually *feel* his son expressing to Francis *Will you sit with me, give me some new company, and watch me play this game, while it takes my mind off of Mommy?* Francis had her own motherly intuition and appreciated how Connor had lightened the burden on Captain's heart. "You've got a new game? I'd love to see it!" Francis said excitedly. Captain directed Francis to sit in the other game chair next to his, as he unpaused the game. He began excitedly playing it while he explained to her what he was doing. She oohed and aahed in all the right places. Connor leaned on the door jamb, watching. He smiled his first genuine smile since Alexis' passing. It may have been Captain's happiest time since then as well. More like his mother, and less like Connor in that respect, Captain loved interacting with people. Connor watched them for a few more minutes, and then he left the two, as he headed back to the living room.

Connor was once again in his recliner when Francis returned to the living room about an hour later. Connor smiled and said, "Thank you for that." Francis returned the smile. "Are you kidding? I had a blast watching him. He kept me involved with what was going on most of the time. It was only the last few minutes that he became so involved with the game, he had stopped explaining to me what was happening. He told me goodbye when I was leaving his room, and then went right back to playing." she said. "I love video games myself, but sometimes I'm guilty of the negative attributes that come along with them as well. I will either let them take too much of my time, or I will let them take too much of his when we could both be doing some other activities." Connor admitted. "As the saying goes, *moderation is best.*" she said. "This is so true." said Connor, looking at Francis. He could see she had something else on her mind.

"Connor, you know I like you, right? You'd say we were friends?" Francis asked. "Well, yeah, I guess so." he said. "And I absolutely love Captain and Alexis." she said. "I believe that." Connor said, starting to feel uneasy with the direction the conversation seemed to be heading. "Well . . ." Francis began but did not complete her thought. She just looked at Connor, as if waiting for him to speak. There was an uncomfortable silence in the room and the mood seemed to be changing. "Say what's on your mind, Francis." said Connor, blatantly. Francis hesitated, momentarily. "Connor, Alexis would be so ashamed of you! Look at yourself! Look at your house! Look at your son!" she finally snapped. "Well, excuse me! I suppose when *your* loved ones die, you would just keep on truckin' with life, as usual, a big smile on your face, while whistling your favorite show tunes!" yelled Connor. "Of course, I wouldn't! I can't possibly imagine what losing the love of your life feels like! But you've got to pull it together, Connor!" Francis yelled back at him. "There's nothing wrong with the way we're living! A few dirty dishes and clothes? Anyway, I thought you were a teacher, not a social worker!" Connor yelled. "A few? And it's not just the dishes and clothes! It's your lives! How are you even supporting yourselves now? You had better be glad that I'm not a social worker!" Francis yelled. "Just leave. Go call Social Services if that's what you want to do." said Connor, calmly. "Connor, I'm not going to do that, I just want to help you in any way that I can . . ." Francis began when Connor interrupted her. "Please, just go." he said. Without another word, Francis left.

After Francis had left the house, Connor lowered his head into his hands and began to cry. For once, he was thankful that Captain kept his gaming volume as loud as he did. Between the volume level and the distance from the living room to the mancave, Connor knew that Captain would not have heard the exchange between him and Francis. He cried harder now than when his wife had passed away. It was as if he was not only feeling the grief of her passing but every little thing that had gone wrong since she had first been diagnosed. It was all rushing in on him at once. He felt terrible about the way he had spoken to Francis. He was so defensive because he knew that she was right, and the guilt and shame from that was bearing down on him as well. She had only been there as a friend, trying to motivate him to work on rebuilding their lives in the absence of Alexis, and he had repaid her by yelling and telling her to leave. Connor extended his recliner all the way back and turned on his side. He buried his face in the crook of his arm as he let months and months of grief flow from his eyes. Whether one would call it a sixth sense, or the father-son telepathy that Connor so enjoyed joking about, another perfect example surfaced. As Connor was feeling the lowest he had ever felt in his life, a short, but strong set of arms lovingly encompassed him, along with a kiss on the top of his head.

| 13 |

Chapter 13: Reboot

Although Connor had not been getting up these days, he still had no need for an alarm. As always, the following morning, his eyes opened early. This time, however, he did not close them back. He woke Captain up, although Captain was not very happy about it. "Good morning, Big Guy. Get up, buddy, we've got a lot to do today." Connor told his son, after kissing him on the forehead. He got up out of bed, went to the kitchen, and started his coffee brewing. He got his vitamins and Captain's medicines ready, and then prepared them a simple breakfast. He carried everything into his bedroom on a TV tray and then had to wake Captain again. Part of their "thing" was Captain feigning the need for assistance getting up out of bed. He grabbed his son's extended arm and pulled him to a sitting position. Captain was always very adamant about trying to find out the details about what was planned out for his day. "Go where?" Captain asked. "I don't think we're going anywhere today, but for starters, we're going to get this house cleaned up from top to bottom." said Connor. Captain just nodded to Connor's response, but he could see the reservation in his son's eyes from just the mention of cleaning up.

Connor sat the TV tray down on the bed. The father and son took their supplements and medications, and then ate breakfast. It took most of the day to get the house back to at least a standard he knew Alexis would have found to be acceptable. Captain was a very big help to his dad. Although sometimes he would take initiative to do chores on his own, usually he had to be told or reminded to do the things that were necessary for living. Connor believed that his son was much smarter than maybe someone who didn't know him would give him credit for. He sometimes wondered if Captain played him. Not in a bad way, of course, but sometimes using his DS to his advantage and steering things in his direction. Some things that Captain did not know how to do; he would learn if you took the time to show him how. Like anyone learning something new, it would take practice. It sometimes just took a little more practice and a little longer for Captain to get the hang of something. It also took patience from the teacher.

Captain smiled a genuine, vibrant smile that Connor hadn't seen in a good while. He had caked on much more shaving cream on Captain's beard than necessary and called him *Captain Claus*. That smile meant everything to Connor. His mind drifted back to the bubble baths they had taken together in their big, garden tub. They would both take the foam bubbles and make beards and hairstyles on each other.

Even before Alexis' passing, Connor had many hard days, for many different reasons, as many people do. He had always made it his mission to try his best to push through those bad days and keep that smile on his son's face. Over the past few weeks, he had guiltily admitted to himself that he had failed that mission. He was bound and determined that he would never fail that mission again. After they both had shaves and haircuts, they took a "light-up shower" together, which consisted of showering by the light of glowsticks that Connor kept on hand for his son's enjoyment. During these "light-up showers," as they bathed, sometimes they would bump heads, which made them both laugh. They also had a special kiss in the middle of the water stream. Connor had fond memories of showering with his son, as he had always tried to make average, ordinary, or even mundane events exciting, or at the very least, more interesting. When Captain was very young, they would take "space showers." The shower was the rocket ship that would take them to a planet full of dinosaurs and treasure to be plundered. One day, when Connor had gotten home from work, he had a homemade coloring page that read "Thank you for taking space showers" waiting for him. As with almost everything Captain had ever made for him, he still had it.

Alexis and Connor had always wanted Captain to have as normal of a life as possible. This included marriage. Captain, being the loving, social person he was, had always had a girlfriend, even as far back as when he was a child. Alexis and Connor had always told him that he could get married at 40 years old. In actuality, if the right girl came into his life, with like-minded parents, it could be even sooner than that. Connor and Alexis had even discussed selling their home and either buying or building a connecting duplex if that's what it took to give Captain the closest vision of the same American dream that most everyone else had while maintaining close proximity for their own peace of mind. With Alexis gone, Connor was not sure if he could ever be without Captain at his side. Deep down, he knew he would do whatever it was that was best for Captain and made him happy.

Although Connor had forced himself into newfound energy, much like the energy he had before Alexis had passed, he still took advantage of the convenience of having some groceries and necessities delivered, instead of having to go out for them. He knew he was eventually going to have to go through Alexis' things and thin the bulk of them out, but he wasn't quite ready for that. He felt as though he and Captain had climbed a mountain just by getting the house presentable and their appearances acceptable once again. He planned to start exercising with Captain and getting him out and about, around people again, as soon as he could. Connor knew if he didn't figure out his work and the financial situation soon, he was going to be in trouble. Although adult day care was affordable in North Carolina, and there were probably some government programs that Captain would qualify for, Connor's biggest concern was trust. He knew of some fine facilities and was 99% sure Captain would be taken care of. However, because both he and Alexis had trust issues when it came to their son, that 1% was a deal-breaker. There were always the news stories of special needs, elder, and child abuse at facilities. Yes, it was rare, but, yes, it did happen. There were only a few people they could really trust with Captain. Alexis' parents, were both gone and Connor's parents, were now barely able to care of themselves. They had a few friends they could trust, but their lives were way too busy. There was one possible person remaining.

Francis had said that she had wanted to help. Well, that was before he basically threw her out of their home. He had already planned an apology for her. What he had said and done to her was wrong, and hopefully, she would find it in her heart to forgive him. He was going to ask her for that help she had been offering, but he certainly wasn't going to blame her if she didn't give it to him. He wasn't even going to blame her if she didn't forgive him.

Unlike Connor, and really the rest of the planet, Alexis' had not been one to embrace the smartphone. She kept all of her contact information in one of those mini-calendar books, that also had an address book section, that she had carried in her pocketbook. He retrieved her pocketbook from their closet where it had sat since she had come home from the hospital. He sat on the bed, and somewhat uncomfortably began digging through her purse. He had always been taught it was not polite to go through a woman's purse. Connor had always wondered why there had seemed to have always been so much emphasis placed on this issue. He felt that *no one* should go through *any* other person's belongings. It didn't take him long to find the calendar book, as it was in the middle of the main compartment. Connor opened the cover and tears immediately welled up in his eyes. On the inside cover, she had written "Connor" and "Captain" and drawn a heart around it. He forcefully, almost angrily, held the tears back and began turning the pages of the calendar. Although his wife had been a teacher at a university, he knew her better than anyone. *Francis Herndon.* Connor thought. Instead of turning to the H section of the address book, he went straight to the F section. Sure enough, there was Francis Herndon's name with a little smiley face beside it. Connor retrieved the cordless phone from the base on the bedside nightstand. With slight apprehension, he dialed the number. After four rings, he heard the voicemail message. "Hi! You've reached Francis Herndon's phone. I can't take this call right now, but if you'd leave me a brief message, I will return your call as soon as I can. 'Bye!" Connor almost hung up, as he felt like he didn't deserve forgiveness from her. *But SHE deserved an apology from him.* he thought. "Francis . . . uhhh . . . look, I wouldn't really blame you for never talking to me again . . . but please call me back . . . I'm very sorry for my behavior, and I'd like to make it up to you . . . Please call me. 'Bye." Connor said, then hung up the phone.

After preparing supper for Captain and himself, Connor went to his home office and began browsing some of the employment sites. He was hoping to find something that he could either do from home or somewhere that would allow Captain to come with him. The university that Alexis had worked at was awesome in that respect. Captain had gone with Connor to work on several occasions when he worked for the police force, but only during times that he had known there was not going to be any activity that could have endangered him. Although there was definitely no shortage of employment opportunities, there was just not a good fit for Connor's life. He was now regretting leaving the department. He knew that under the circumstances, Captain Lester would have worked with him somehow to make it work. If not by Captain being with him at the desk job, but possibly another job that would have worked out even better for Captain to be with him. Being the man that Captain Lester was, he felt as if he would still do what he could to help him. Once you left the department, there was usually a slim chance of coming back. Connor had seen this over the years. He had even been surprised by a few of the employees that they had not taken back. He knew the department he worked for was about as nonpartisan as you could get these days. But he knew that Captain Lester's word carried a lot of weight. It could all depend on what he thought of Connor. He was reaching for the cordless phone, when it rang, startling him.

"Hi, Connor, it's Francis." she said. "Oh, Francis, thank you for calling me back. I just wanted to tell you how sorry I am for the way I treated you. Can you find it in your heart to forgive me?" Connor asked. "Connor, I'm not going to lie, I was really upset. But I didn't really hold it against you. I can only imagine what you've been through. I know you're going to be dealing with this pain you're feeling for the rest of your life. I was, of course, concerned about what was going to happen to you and Captain before the pain was soft enough for you to function once again. I just wanted to help." she said. "I realize that now, and probably subconsciously did then, I guess I was just hurting too much to process any constructive criticism."

said Connor. "I understand, Connor. I do forgive you." said Francis. "Thank you, Francis. That really means a lot." said Connor. He hesitated. He didn't want to follow his apology with a plea for help. *I'll just call Captain Lester and see what he might be able to do for me.* Connor thought. "Well, I won't hold you up, Francis, I know you have work to do. Thank you for calling me back. I just had to let you know how sorry I was." Connor finished. It was Francis' turn to hesitate. "Connor, I know you need help with Captain, and I know you're too proud to ask, especially after what happened. I can help you Connor. He can come with me to the university just as he did with Alexis if that's what you would like. You would just have to work around my schedule as well, on days that I may not be able to keep him for whatever reason." she said. Connor was almost in tears. After the way he had treated her, she was not only willing to help him, she had actually *volunteered* to do so. "How did you know?" Connor asked, his voice slightly cracking. "Alexis and I talked about everything. I probably know some things about you that you'd rather I didn't." said Francis with a laugh. "Alexis had always talked about how special you are. I always liked you, but now I know what she meant. You don't know what this means to me. Would you and David be willing to come to our house for dinner this Friday?" he asked. "I would love to come and I know David would, too." she said. "Great! It can be a "thank you" dinner and we can work out the details for Captain going with you. Would 6 o'clock work?" asked Connor with relief in his voice. "That would be perfect. We'll be there!" said Francis.

"Thank you, Francis." said Connor. "You're very welcome." They said their goodbyes, then hung up.

| **14** |

Chapter 14: God is in the Details

Friday had arrived, and the Gellar men had worked hard for many hours to prepare a delicious bounty for their guests. Grilled chicken, sauteed asparagus, tossed salad, dinner rolls, and mashed potatoes for Captain, of course. They used their best dinnerware and set the table as properly as they knew how. Unlike the Gellars, the Herndons seemed to always be punctual. Captain answered the door when they arrived. He greeted and hugged them both. David and Francis followed Captain into the dining room just as Connor was placing the last serving dish on the table. "Hello, Connor." said David. "Hi, David . . . how have you been?" said Connor, looking up from the table at the Herndons as they filed into the room behind Captain. "I have my good days and my bad days. Fortunately, today is a good one, with only some mild issues and pain. Unfortunately, the bad days are starting to outnumber the good ones." said David. Connor looked at Francis questioningly. "Connor, David has Parkinson's Disease." she said, bluntly. Connor's eyebrows went up in surprise. David looked over at Francis, also surprised. "I'm sorry, David, I didn't know anything about it." said Connor. Both David and Connor were looking at Francis expectantly. "Of course, I had shared your condition with Alexis, she is one of my best friends, but I told her not to mention it to anyone. You know how you like your privacy, David. I can see that she did indeed keep it to herself. I'm sorry if you feel you had been left out of something, Connor." Francis said, directing her comments to both David and Connor. "No, no, that's quite alright. I do understand. Alexis and I did share just about everything, but in this case, it was not her place to share that." said Connor. "Well, enough about me . . . Francis tells me that you've had an understandably rough time and need some help and that she is going to be able to help you." said David. "Yes, let's all sit down and start eating dinner while it's hot, and then we can talk about that afterward." said Connor.

Captain comically smacked his lips as they all took their seats. "Son, would you like to say the blessing?" Connor asked. Francis and David held their hands out, then Captain and Connor extended theirs, and they all held hands. They all closed their eyes and bowed their heads. "Father God, thank you for the food. Thank you for our friends, Francis and David. Thank you for my daddy. And, Lord, please watch over Mommy. Amen." said Captain. "Amen." said Connor, David, and Francis, concurrently. Connor pushed away the wave of emotions that washed over him from Captain praying for his mother, and he believed Francis was doing the same thing. "Good job, Son." he said, thankfully keeping his voice from cracking.

Connor had already pureed Captain's chicken, and mixed in the necessary ketchup and ranch dressing to give it the texture and consistency that he liked and was used to. Captain had gotten choked on a few occasions during his life, with one experience of a good Samaritan performing the Heimlich maneuver to save his life. The man that had saved Captain had said it was as if God had taken over his body, controlled his actions and had taken him through the motions. Connor did not doubt this, and still gets emotional when he thinks about it. These scary events had made it hard for Connor and Alexis to put their hearts into the efforts for him to learn to chew properly. He had a few eating therapies over the years but had made only a little progress. They had both known that continuing to puree his food was not necessarily helping Captain, especially with their desire for him to be as self-sufficient as possible, but the risks of choking had kept them on edge.

The four of them had a nice time during dinner. They all exchanged some stories and items of interest from each of their lives. Francis had told some comical events involving Alexis that had happened at the university. Although there was a gentle ache without her there, it was nice to hear some positive and comical memories that involved her. Some-times, Captain would seem to be upset when others laughed about some things that he didn't understand, but Francis had told her stories specifically so that he would. In some of the stories she told, Captain was a part of what happened. He really loved to hear about things he had been involved with. It warmed Connor's heart to see his son smile and to hear that magical laugh.

After dinner, because Connor needed to work out some details with Francis, Captain was happy to have David follow him to his mancave and get a first-hand demonstration of his new game, as Francis had. Francis helped Connor begin to clear the table and clean up the dining room and kitchen. "You have really turned things around, Connor." said Francis, referring to the order and cleanliness of the house. "Really, thanks to you." he said. "I'd like to think that I helped to motivate you, but I think you would have eventually pulled yourself up." she said. "Maybe. It's still very hard." Connor said. "I know it is. You'll still have bad days . . . just remember to try not to let it keep you down long. For your sake, but mostly for Captain's." she said, smiling. "I'm going to do my best." he said. "When I had told you that I didn't know how you felt when I had come over before, I had lied to you, Connor. I wanted to help you, but I was also scared of bringing up my past heartache. Because I have been exactly where you are now, I really do know how you feel and what you've been going through." said Francis. "You were married before?" Connor asked as he was scraping leftovers from a plate into the trashcan. Francis was rinsing the scraped dishes in the sink, then placing them into the dish-washing machine. "Yes, I was. I do love David with all my heart, but I also loved my first husband, Kyle. You've heard the term *whirlwind romance,* and this was definitely one of them. He was twenty-two, the same age as Captain is now, and I was only nineteen when we got married. We had only been married three years when Kyle was killed in a car wreck. I can honestly say when we first got married, maybe our hormones had driven us more in a carnal nature, but after three years of marriage, we had grown to know a love like nothing else." Francis said, with a forlorn look in her eyes. "So, does David know about Kyle?" Connor asked in a low voice, as he glanced at the kitchen entrance closest to Captain's mancave. "Oh, my, yes. And he's been married before, also. He knows all about Kyle and what Kyle means to me. There's no shame in loving someone, and then loving someone else in those circumstances." she said.

After they were finished cleaning up, Connor asked Francis to the living room and treated them to some coffee and chocolate chip cookies. "Francis, try to keep the yelling to a minimum this time." Connor said, jokingly. Francis chuckled as she sat her coffee cup on the saucer. "So, how long has David had Parkinson's?" Connor asked. "He was diagnosed about 6 years ago when he first started having mild tremors. His doctor said he is in stage 3." she said. "I'm sorry I don't really know anything about Parkinson's. Is that bad?" Connor asked. "It's okay, most people don't know a lot about illnesses and such unless they directly affect their own families. There are pretty much 5 stages of Parkinson's. Stage 4 is when you basically begin to lose the ability to take care of yourself. Your abilities and the severity of the disease will vary from person to person. David has actually been doing very well." said Francis. "I'm very sorry you two are having to deal with this. Are you sure about taking on the responsibility of Captain? It's not going to be too much on you?" Connor asked. "Oh, heavens no. As David said, he has good days and bad days, but he's still able to take care of himself. He can still drive and do everything anyone else can. Sometimes he may choose not to go out on one of his worse days, but there's always been a good day around the corner." she said.

"Well, if you're sure. And I don't expect you to do this for free." said Connor. "Look, I don't mind. I don't expect anything. But if you insist, at least wait until you get caught back up. Then, as you feel you are able, you can give me whatever you think is fair." she said. "Thank you, Francis. So what do I need to do? Meet you at your home in the mornings?" asked Connor. "Goodness no! I know you want to make things convenient for me, but we can meet at the store at Gonzalee street where there's easy access off of and then back onto the interstate. That would be on your way to downtown, and I can jump back onto the interstate to continue heading to the university." she said. "That would work perfectly! What time would you want to meet there?" asked Connor. "Let's go with 8:30am, that will give me plenty of time to get to the university before nine. You can set your own hours, right?" she asked. "Yes, that time would be perfect and thank you for thinking of a convenient meeting place for the both of us. Choosing my time is one of my few benefits. I need to call Mr. Horowitz to see if my old office is still available. I'll try to catch him this weekend. If it's available, I'll go ahead and see if he'll let me have it back this Monday. I'm going to contact some of my old clients to let them know I'm back and maybe they will help me spread the word. I can also get some exposure by letting everyone know that I'm back on social media. I can advertise in the Edmonton Edition, but they won't be out until Wednesday. It may be a slow week starting, but if it's anything like before, business will be booming in no time." said Connor, slightly excited. "Oh, and I hope this is not an inconvenience for you, but I always only schedule half a day of work on Fridays. I don't mind at all bringing him to your office or home, whatever works for you around lunch-time on Fridays. I know that there may be some evenings you may need to work in the line of work you do, and I may be able to help you out then, also, but you need to give me as much notice as possible. And another thing, I can't help you on weekends. That's our time, David and I. And remember, there may be a day here and there throughout the regular week that you may have to work around my schedule if there are certain events, functions, doctors' appointments and so on that would keep me from having Captain with me." said Francis. "Francis, you have given me way more than I could ever have hoped for. I am very grateful." Connor said, with sincerity.

The four friends said their goodbyes. It was starting to get late, and Connor was always a believer in *early to bed, early to rise.* Connor had Captain sit down in the living room, so he could talk to him. "Did you have fun tonight?" Connor asked. "Yep." Captain said. "Did you enjoy David's company?" Connor asked. "Yep." responded Captain. "Did you let David play any?" Connor asked. "No, he don't like to play the game. He watch me." said Captain. "But you still had fun with him, right?" asked Connor. "Uh-huh." said Captain. "That's good. David and Francis are good people, aren't they?" Connor asked. Captain nodded and said "I love Francis!" said Captain. "That's good, Captain. How would you like to go with Francis to school as you did with Mommy?" asked Connor. Captain thought about it for a few moments. "To Mommy's school?" Captain asked. "Yes, to Mommy's school, but with Francis to *her* class." said Connor. Captain thought about it momentarily and then said "Mm-hmm." Connor smiled. "Awesome, Captain! You ready for bed, big boy?" Connor asked. "Yep. I get my snacks." said Captain.

Captain got his favorite brand of yogurt, some chocolate milk, and two drinkable yogurts that he had started sharing with his dad. They watched one of their favorite science fiction shows, as they had their snacks. Connor loved the show and was happy to be watching it with his son, but he found it difficult to follow the storyline, as he was thinking of all the preparations he was going to have to make in order to give his PI business another go. Captain had taken melatonin and Connor had taken something a little more powerful as a sleep aid that night, and both fell asleep during their show.

Connor got himself and Captain up early, and after having his coffee, they worked out in their home gym that shared space with the dining room. Connor, of course, had to walk for his cardio, due to his bum leg, but he was still able to work out every other body part. Breakfast for Connor was simply a protein shake that he split with Captain. Captain usually had protein and yogurt. They showered, and Connor let Captain do what he wanted to do, which was usually play video games or watch some of his favorite shows. As a game lover himself, he had absolutely no problem with that, as long as Captain was getting proper diet and exercise along with it. Sometimes, Captain would ask for a custom coloring page that Connor was more than happy to do on the computer.

Connor's first order of business for the day was to see if Mr. Horowitz was available by phone. Fortune would have it, that not only did he get Mr. Horowitz, but Connor's old office had not been rented out. Everything was still as it was. Being the nice guy Mr. Horowitz was, he did not ask for a deposit, he told Connor that he could pay the first month's rent next month. Connor then proceeded to his social media account. He posted that his investigative service was back in business and made sure to put the address for his office and his cellphone number. He did not know the process for suspending an account of someone that was deceased and had not had the heart to look into it yet. He did know that he was friends with several of Alexis' friends on social media, so they would see the post for his business as well. He could use every opportunity for advertisement that was available. Otherwise, he and Captain were going to be looking for a smaller home or an apartment. While he was on the computer, he went ahead and looked up the Edmonton Edition newspaper website. Sure enough, you could sign up for an ad online. He used his credit card and placed a quarter-page ad, using a file that he had edited from where they had advertised before, putting the updated starting date. He knew the paper would still not come out until Wednesday, but at least this was one more item he had accomplished. After he was done using the computer, he retrieved his cellphone. He thought for a few moments, then popped open the text editor on his phone. After many minutes of thinking about it and several revisions, he finally came up with:

Hello, Friend,
You are receiving this text, because you have
been a valued client of Gellar Investigative
Services. Some of you know that I have endured
an unfortunate loss in my family and I had needed
to take a substantial amount of time away from my
business. I just wanted to let you know that I am
now back and I am ready to serve you in any of
your investigative needs. If you should again
need any of my services, I would appreciate your
consideration. If you do not, I would also be
grateful if you would refer me to your friends or
associates that may be in need of such services.
Thank you and I wish you the best,
Connor Gellar.
Gellar Investigative Services

Once Connor had been satisfied with the wording of his text, he copied and pasted the text into text messages that he sent out to many clients with whom he had contact numbers on his cellphone. Although he knew it may not amount to anything by way of actually making a difference in his advertising effort, he was pleasantly surprised when most of the clients he had texted had responded to him. They were all positive responses, acknowledging his request, and a few had even inquired about how he was doing. These small gestures meant the world to Connor right now.

Chapter 15: Gellar Investigative Services: Reprise

Connor gave his son a kiss on the lips, something he could not even remember doing with his own father, and then a big hug. He placed Captain's backpack and lunch box in the back seat of Francis' car, as Captain got into the front seat. "Thank you, Francis. I hope you both have a great day!" Connor said. Captain smiled at his dad and Francis said "You too, Connor, good luck!" The car headed down the road toward the interstate exit. Connor got back into his car, and headed for his office.

When Connor arrived at his office, he noticed a seemingly familiar car parked in one of the two spaces that were actually allotted for his office. There was also a person standing in front of and facing his office door. As he pulled into the spot next to it and could see the car closer, the person turned around confirming his initial thoughts. Connor's heart sped up and he could feel his face beginning to flush. It was Daniel. Connor's emotions were in jumbles. This man had literally saved his life, but could that one event make up for the fact that he basically deserted him during the toughest times of his life and during his greatest need. His mind was flashing with a multitude of choices of things he would say to Daniel from the categories of *1) just keep it business-like, 2) be the bigger man and ask how Daniel is doing,* or *3) tear into him with a fierce tongue-lashing.*

Connor got out of his car, closed the door, and pressed the lock button. Connor surprised himself by not choosing from any of the categories his mind had initially provided him. He walked past Daniel without giving him a second glance, un-locked his office door, and walked in, leaving Daniel staring after him. He justified his heedlessness toward Daniel with the old adage *If you can't say something nice, don't say anything at all.* Connor couldn't help but wonder if ignoring Daniel would give him the incentive to leave, or would he now want to come into the office to talk to him. Connor couldn't lie to himself, he was definitely curious as to why Daniel aban-doned him not only when he had left the force, but when his wife had passed away, and during the tough times that had followed. Ultimately, though, as he was contentedly already receiving texts actually hiring him with the details provided for the services needed, some texts requesting in-person meetings, and some texts simply inquiring about pricing, he couldn't afford to spend time or energy concentrating on whatever excuses Daniel had to give him or whatever guilt he wished to relinquish.

Connor hung his jacket up on a hook on the wall. He started the coffee maker, turned on his computer, laid out a notepad, pencil, and his cellphone on his desk, and then sat down. He began writing notes from his phone's text messages on his notepad when his inner office door opened and Daniel walked in. Connor looked up at him from his work and stared for a few moments, thinking more about what he might say. He finally asked "Can I help you?" as flatly and emotionlessly as possible. Daniel walked closer to Connor's desk and said "I hope so."

Connor inhaled deeply and then let his breath go out through his nose. He made sure the sound produced by his exhalation was loud enough for Daniel to hear, and yet soft enough so that this familiar sound of being disturbed, interrupted, or inconvenienced seemed genuine. "What do you want?" Connor asked, putting on an air of impatience. Daniel knew Connor all too well to know that he was going to have to work hard on his apology. Connor was the best and most trusted man he knew. Once you were Connor's friend, if you were in need, the man would do anything he could to help you. Back when Connor's life was changed forever by that shotgun blast to the leg, it was not just because Daniel had been a cop and the man's partner. Having Connor's selfless friendship was equally motivating to save his life. Daniel had no doubt whatsoever that if he would have had to put himself between the shotgun and Connor in order to save his life, he would have done so, without hesitation. With all that said, however, as Daniel had seen firsthand on more than one occasion throughout the years, once you had fallen out of Connor's good graces, there was no coming back. Not that there had not been times when Connor had been hurt or slighted, then there had been an apology offered, and Connor had accepted it. Cordiality and a working relationship had been maintained, but there had never been a real reconciliation and the friendships or relationships were never quite the same again. As his partner, Daniel had even joked with Connor and compared him to the *woman scorned* proverb on one occasion. As if to further prove Daniel's humorous point, Connor did not like the reference at all, and Daniel had learned not to bring that particular matter up again. If this was even something considered a character flaw, it would only have been one of a few, with all of Connor's good characteristics vastly outnumbering the bad ones. From that point forward, as Daniel truly cherished Connor's friendship, he would dance around the line with any tomfoolery or bantering with Connor, but never cross it. He could tell from Connor's demeanor that he had not only crossed the line by great margins but understandably left a chasm in its place. It was Daniel's hope that he could repair their friendship, and that his explanation for needing help would assist him in doing so.

"First of all, Connor, let me say how very sorry I am about Alexis . . ." began Daniel. Even with his bum leg, Connor surprised Daniel when he had quickly jumped up to a standing position at his desk. The motion of standing so fast had launched the back of his knees against the front of his rolling chair and had thrown it into the wall behind him with a loud bang. "No!" Connor yelled. "I don't want *your* sympathy, Daniel! She wasn't just your ex-partner's wife, she was *your friend*, too!" Connor continued, yelling loudly. All the way back to when Connor and Daniel wore blue uniforms, and even before they had become partners, they had become friends. Both the Gellar and Bryson families would have supper at each other's homes from time to time, the Bryson's twin boy and girl had loved to play with Captain growing up, and they had all even went on some vacations together. Their wives weren't the bosom buddies that Connor and Daniel were, but had enough in common to enjoy each other's company. Of course, Connor had told Alexis about Daniel standing him up for the farewell lunch, but beyond that, he had not communicated with her any more about him. He had done his best to put on a brave face that Daniel's abandonment of their friendship had not even bothered him. Surely, Alexis had noticed Daniel's absence when she got sick. Not one visit or even a single phone call. Connor would have thought that even Daniel's wife would have at least phoned to check on her and see if the family needed anything.

"I know, Connor, and I'm sorry . . ." Daniel had tried to speak again, very loudly. "I don't want your sympathy and I don't want your apology and I don't want your excuses!" Connor yelled, interrupting Daniel. Connor's face had turned red and his voice was starting to get hoarse from yelling. Connor picked up the pencil and notepad he had been jotting notes on before Daniel walked in. He tore half a page from the sheet on the bottom of the pad. He opened up his contacts on his cellphone that was lying on his desk. He began to write on the scrap of paper he had torn from the notepad. "I don't understand why a police detective would need the help of a private investigator, but just in case you're not here trying to also pile some lies on top of your tower of sympathies, apologies, and excuses for your good, ole pal, here's the name, number and address of the next closest PI to Edmonton." snapped Connor. He slapped the piece of paper on his desk, closest to where Daniel was standing. Daniel slowly lowered his gaze to the scrap of paper. He saw the name, number, and address for a PI. The address was in the town of Dernmont, about half an hour east of Edmonton. Daniel had a feeling that if he retrieved that scrap of paper and walked out that door, it would most likely be the last time he would ever see or speak to his friend again. He didn't know what to do or say. His situation was dire and he needed help badly. He did not want to lose his longtime friend, either.

Daniel did not retrieve the scrap of paper from Connor's desk. He turned away from Connor and slowly walked to the door. He grasped the doorknob, turned it, and then opened the door. He stood there momentarily, holding the door open. Daniel Began speaking softly in the hopes that Connor would not interrupt him. "Do you remember that case we worked on about three years ago, when we arrested a husband for beating his wife? She had a black eye and some bruises on her face. He claimed that he didn't do it and there was no trace of any of his wife's DNA on his hands to prove that he did, not that he could not have done a perfect job of cleaning them. All of the people we had interviewed, even the wife's friends, had nothing but good things to say about him. We know better than most, that people aren't always who they seem to be. And so does Captain Lester. That's why he said that case was closed and that it could be worked out in the court system. But from having spoken to the husband and wife, you and I both had a hunch that this case was not so cut and dried. Against Captain Lester's judgment, we staked out the couple's home the same night that we had arrested the husband. Sure enough, very late in the night, a man showed up at their house. This, of course, led to reopening the case, and after some of our excellent police work, we eventually proved that she had self-inflicted the trauma to her face simply because she wanted to be with another man. You could never possibly forget that one, could you, Connor?" Daniel finished. He waited for Connor's response, and there was none. "Connor, Officer Harris - Rachel - is not who you think she is. I messed up and now I'm in a world of trouble. I stand to lose everything." Daniel added. Connor still did not speak. Daniel proceeded through the open door as Connor had finally simply said the word "Wait."

Connor had not said another word to Daniel, but he had rolled the top sheet of his notepad over, curling it to the back, and picked up his pencil. He wrote "DB" at the top of the clean sheet, along with the date and time. Connor had not only remained silent; he had also not made any motions or gestures to Daniel. Daniel took it upon himself to sit in one of the chairs in front of Connor's desk, facing him. After having written Daniel's initials, with the date and time, Connor held the pencil above the empty first line of the notepad sheet and looked up at Daniel, expectantly. Rather than try to apologize again, Daniel had simply decided to start at the beginning of when his trouble first began. If Connor was willing to listen to Daniel's problem with Rachel, then there was at least hope that his explanation would open the door to salvage their friendship. All he could do is tell Connor everything that had happened and hope for the best.

"Right after our incident, Connor, they knew it was going to be a while before you could return as my partner. No one really knew that you wouldn't be coming back to the field at all at that time. They posted your position as a temporary one. Rachel applied immediately and was given the job. At the time, when she first started working with me, I didn't really think anything of it. This was her first assignment as a detective. Of course, she was going to be excited. We all are, when we first start, right? But it seemed that there was something a little more than just excitement. It seemed to be even deeper than just the new employee following the experienced one like a puppy dog. Almost immediately, she began telling me how she had always had a crush on me. She had told me how she had been so disappointed that she had not made detective sooner, so that maybe, somehow, someway, she could get partnered with me. The conversations were starting to get a little too personal, and weirder and weirder by the day. I had tried to be respectful and I certainly didn't want to alienate her or make her feel uncomfortable around me, but I knew I was going to have to try to get her to pump the brakes. We had some surveillance to do one night, and I could tell something was different about her. It was as if she had already prepared for us to have some sort of *romantic* evening together instead of police work. While we were in the parked car in the dark, she kissed me. I gently pushed her away and I told her that I was a happily married man and had two kids in college. It didn't seem to faze her. Some of our surveillance subjects came out of the house we were parked in front of, and Rachel took that opportunity to continue trying to seduce me. She knew that I wouldn't create a disturbance or make a scene with our surveillance subjects so close to us. One thing led to another . . ." said Daniel. Connor had been filling pages on his notepad. He finished his last note and then looked at Daniel.

"Why didn't you immediately report this to the captain?" asked Connor. "Come on Connor, I'm not even sure whether you believe me or not! I'm 20 years older than her and she is prettier than the prettiest girl I dated when I was in my prime. I know Captain Lester wouldn't believe me! But I swear it's the truth! She told me that if I ever told anyone, not only would she tell my wife, but she would make sure the whole world knew. I would lose my wife, my kids would hate me, and I would lose my job. Just imagine the implications to the department. Since that night, she has basically been controlling me and using me as some sort of twisted personal consort." said Daniel. "Why didn't you come to me *sooner?* Why did you wait so long? Obviously, you were enjoying the attention and the situation." said Connor. "I'm not going to lie, I was of course flattered and enjoyed the attention, but what man wouldn't have been?" asked Daniel. "I don't know, maybe a *faithful, honorable man?*" asked Connor, sarcastically.

"I *never* wanted this to happen. Right after you announced that you were leaving, she basically *forbid* me to contact you again. I guess she knew you would interfere. I had already begun seeing her whenever and wherever she wanted and was getting wound tighter and tighter into her spider's web." said Daniel, pausing for a breath. "I have had to lie to my wife whenever Rachel keeps me out and I've had to lie to Rachel just to try to do *anything*. I've become a pro at lying! But, Connor, I swear, I'm not lying to you now, and I need some help!" said Daniel, placing his face in his hands, his body slightly shaking. He had never seen his tough, confident partner this vulnerable. After a moment, Connor asked. "Were you at Alexis' graveside service?" Daniel slowly lifted his head from his hands. "Yes, I was there briefly, near the end of the service, and I left right after it. Rachel was expecting me. I get by with what I can." said Daniel. "I thought I saw you." said Connor. "Look, I feel like terrible. But I'm telling you, not just because of her infatuation with me or whatever you want to call it, there's something really off with this woman. The more I get to know her outside of the mask she wears for everyone else, the more I'm seriously worried about what she might end up doing." said Daniel.

"So why now?" asked Connor. "Her demands on me are getting out of hand. And she seems to be getting stranger by the minute. She's starting to get upset whenever I have to go home. I'm getting exhausted telling all these lies and living this double life. This has to stop, but I don't want to lose *everything*. I don't know if you can help me or not, but I've got to do something, Connor." said Daniel. "How were you able to get away today, to meet with me?" asked Connor. "Well, I'm a little embarrassed to tell you this, but I have to tell you the truth. We usually go to that little motel off Highway 4." said Daniel. Connor was stunned and Daniel knew that this revelation would throw him for a loop. It was the same motel where Connor had been shot and Daniel had killed the man. "Unbelievable." Connor said. "I know, I know. I'm telling you, Connor, I really think she likes being close to where that violence had happened. When we went there today, I made like we were going to party, and I offered her a stimulant that I had taken from evidence. I happened to know this particular stimulant would cause her to crash hard and sleep a while afterward. Of course, I pretended to take it, too. But I do need to make sure I'm there when she wakes up." said Daniel. Connor nodded slowly, with understanding. After they sat quietly for a few moments, Connor looked at Daniel with a poker face. "Daniel, I'll do whatever I can to help you. I'm going to have to get started by digging into her past and see what I can find out. Maybe this will give us a better idea of what we're dealing with and help figure out what we're going to do." said Connor. He could see relief wash over Daniel's face. "Thank you, Connor. Not just for agreeing to help me, but for believing me." said Daniel. "What's not to believe? If the prettiest officer on the force is attracted to *you*, there is definitely *something* wrong." said Connor, smiling.

Daniel stood up, walked around the desk, and hugged Connor on his shoulders. "You're not out of the woods just yet. I will do my best, but there's no guarantee that by the end of this thing, everything won't end up out in the open.

You could still lose everything, Daniel. You have to make that choice. If you do nothing, it's probably eventually going to come to a head anyway, as you get into this deeper and deeper. Or, we can try to get to the bottom of it sooner with as little collateral damage as possible, and at least it could become known that you knew you had made a mistake and had tried to rectify it." said Connor. "My choice is to try to get out of it as soon as possible. I agree that on its current trajectory, it's eventually coming out. I can't hold on much longer." said Daniel. Connor nodded. "Can you keep me updated with texts?" Connor asked. "No. Rachel is so paranoid; she is constantly going through my phone." said Daniel. "Okay, buy a burner phone, text me the number, and keep it hidden. As you know, make sure you pay cash, and it wouldn't hurt to disguise your face when you buy it. We'll try to keep this out of the news but be prepared that it may not be possible to do so. Make sure she never finds it or never sees you using it. If we are successful, you can just destroy the phone after everything is said and done." said Connor. "I will get one as soon as possible." said Daniel. "Look, Daniel, I know you can't afford me, especially with the kids away in college, and this double life you've been maintaining, and I don't want to charge a friend, but I've been having a really rough time, financially. You will have to bear with me, as I'm going to have to work on this in-between other cases. For the time being, keep her complacent and don't act any differently than you usually do. Don't give her any reason to be suspicious." said Connor. Daniel was relieved to hear Connor refer to him as a friend once again, and wasn't even sure Connor realized he had called him that. "Keep up with your time, Connor, I will pay you every penny." said Daniel. Connor stood up. "You had better get back to her before she awakens." Connor said. Daniel hugged Connor around the shoulders again, and Connor returned the hug. "Thank you, Connor." said Daniel. "We'll get to the bottom of this, buddy." said Connor. Daniel left.

Connor sat back down at his desk and continued to work. He answered texts, returned phone calls, and scheduled in-person appointments. He began doing research on cases that had hired him with the resources he had available via the internet with the computer in his office. He absolutely had every intention of trying to help Daniel, but what he had told Daniel was the truth. He had to do the work of his paying customers first, and work on Daniel's problem as he had the opportunity. He realized time may be critical, but he had a young man depending on him to keep the lights on. To his relief, the influx of cases was similar in number to when he had first started. It was as if he had never really left. Possibly his lower cost and the convenience of hiring someone locally was good for business. With the services as expensive as they were, any savings a client could make certainly helped them out.

Over the next few weeks, Connor worked very hard, and in those weeks, he had accumulated enough cases to last him for many months. He was even having to give potential clients the choice of being referred to another PI, which was usually the same one that he had been going to send Daniel to, or if they felt their matter could wait, he told them he would get to it later, as he caught up with his other cases. Some would take the referral and some would choose to wait. Through his calls, texts, and in-person interviews, he had received a variety of cases. As usual, most of them were cheating spouses and workers' comp related. However, there were a few unique ones that might prove to be interesting. He had gotten so busy, that he found that he had to lock his outer door and re-hang his flip sign on it that read ***On assignment. Please call and leave a message.*** even when he was actually in his office working, in order to get research and other administration duties performed without constant interruptions. Daniel had finally texted him from a burner phone, simply by texting him "DB" from the strange number that showed up on Connor's cell. Connor had texted back "Got it. I will get back to you as soon as possible."

| 16 |

Chapter 16: A Turn for the Worse and then a Reverse

Another few weeks went by, and Connor was hard at work, using some of his resources on the internet at his office when his cellphone rang. He glanced over at it, getting ready to send the call to voicemail when he saw it was Francis' cell number. She never called. His heart skipped a beat and he grabbed the phone up and answered. "Francis? I'm here. Is something wrong?" he asked, worriedly. "Everything is fine with Captain, so don't worry. But I do need you to pick him up at our house this evening instead of meeting you at our spot." she said. "Ok, I'll leave now." said Connor, standing. "No. no, it's not an emergency, you can finish out your day, just come here, to our house, when you are done." said Francis. "Is everything okay with David?" asked Connor. "I'm afraid not. I'll fill you in when you pick up Captain." she said. "I'm sorry, Francis. I'll get this last little bit of work done and head your way." said Connor. He sat back down at his computer and hurriedly finished some of the tasks he had been working on.

Connor pulled into the Herndon's driveway. He walked up to the front door of the modest, but beautifully maintained home and knocked. Francis answered and asked Connor to come in. She led him into the kitchen and offered him something to drink. "Captain is in the living room watching TV." she said. "Have a seat." she added. Connor sat down at the kitchen table. "Connor, David was in a car wreck today." Francis said, bluntly. "Oh my! Is he hurt? Was anyone else hurt?" Connor asked. "David is fine and no one is hurt. He had to have a sedative, and he's in bed resting. Even though David was supposed to know not to drive, he decided to go get some fast food for lunch today. As far as he made it was to our neighbor's driveway across the street. He backed straight out, up into their driveway, and right into their car." she said. Connor reached across the table and gripped Francis' hand and she returned the squeeze. "I'm so sorry, Francis." said Connor. "I'm the one that's sorry, Connor. I had planned on helping you more. We were already expecting that things like this were going to start happening, but we thought we still had more time before dementia and Parkinson's started to rear their ugly heads together. David is starting to change, Connor. Even with me present, I just wouldn't feel safe having Captain around. There's no telling what he might do. I may be overreacting, but I'd rather not take any chances." said Francis. "Look, you don't need to worry about us, you're going to have your hands full with your own problems now. You have already helped me tremendously, for which I will always be grateful. I will figure something out. We will be fine." said Connor.

The two Gellar men both gave Francis a hug as they prepared to leave. "Francis, don't hesitate to call *me* if *you* were to need some help. I will certainly do what I can." said Connor. "Same here, boys. If there is anything I can do to help, I will. I just wish I could have given you more time." she said. "I know you do, Francis. If it's not Mother Nature spanking us, it's Father Time beating us." said Connor, jokingly. Connor and Captain left by the front door, and Francis turned on the front porch light to provide them some light, as twilight was beginning to transition to dusk. Francis watched them through the storm door until they had both entered the car, and then she closed her front interior door. Once Connor had started the car and the headlights came on, the front porch light winked out. Connor looked over at Captain and lovingly ran his fingers through the back of his hair, cupping his perfect head. "My coconut." said Connor to his son, often referring to his son's head as such. Captain looked at Connor and rubbed his head in a similar manner and said "My cantaloupe." as he smiled at his dad in the soft glow of the car's instrument panel. Connor returned Captain's smile, hoping that it was convincing. He had told Francis that they would be fine. He had told her that he would figure something out. Connor wasn't sure how true either of those statements were. Francis had been his last hope when he had tried to *figure something out* before. *As long as we have each other.* Connor thought, looking at his son once more before checking his rearview mirror, and shifting into reverse. He pulled out of the Herndon's driveway and headed home.

It wasn't a very long drive home and Captain had already begun surfing the internet, playing media, and entertaining himself with his cellphone. This still afforded Connor an opportunity and some time to contemplate his situation. He had a case stakeout planned for tomorrow. He was originally going to see if Francis could keep Captain very late, or possibly allow him to stay the entire night. Even though there were a few friends that would probably be more than happy to help him out, that would only be a temporary fix for their situation. He wasn't going to ask any friends to make such a drastic change in their lives, even if they could. Connor wanted constant supervision and assistance available for Captain at all times. Only people that had been in Connor's shoes and had been in a similar situation would understand this. A stranger watching Captain had never been an option, and it never would be. He would continue to look for jobs that he could possibly do remotely so that Captain could be home with him. He had already tried his luck with that option and had been sadly disappointed. He would just have to try again. He could always look into applying for some sort of disability benefits due to his leg, and Captain's need for twenty-four-hour care. If he was approved, however, he was sure that would mean significantly downsizing their living accommodations, and possibly even having to apply for some sort of government-subsidized housing.

This evening, Connor was happy that Captain wanted to enjoy their supper together while watching one of their favorite shows. Captain usually preferred to watch one of his own favorite shows, alone in their home office. Maybe Captain sensed that Connor needed some emotional support through that special father-son telepathy. He certainly nailed it. Connor's mind couldn't shake the negative feelings he was having this evening. He felt like these could be some of the last family times they spent together in the home that they had shared with Captain's mother. Although the rent was dirt-cheap on his office, Connor knew he could always drop it, and just do his administration and research work from home. He knew that particular change would not look good to his current and prospective clients right now, as it was not that long ago that he had reopened. Mr. Horowitz had been kind enough to forego a deposit and basically had given him a full month for free. He would hold on to it for as long as he could. After supper, Connor and Captain took a light-up shower, and then Connor told him he could go play some of his games until bedtime. He had a feeling Captain was wanting to play, anyway, he had just been hanging with Connor because he sensed that he needed him. It made Connor think of one of his sayings about his special needs son. *He's special, and I need him.*

He let Captain enjoy his many methods of digital entertainment until Connor himself began feeling groggy. He went to Captain's mancave and peeked in before opening the door. Captain was playing a game while listening to music *while* talking to one of his friends on a video chat. Connor himself felt fortunate that he was able to do *one* thing at a time, much less *three*. He had even seen Captain doing all of those things before, while watching a TV show, too.

Although some typical people may be able to accomplish this multi-tasking as well, Connor had never ceased to be amazed at what his son could do. Especially considering the fact that when Captain was born, he and Alexis were pretty much told that their son would not be able to do much of anything. One nurse had even been sure to let them know that *there were places for children like this.* To this day, Connor remained dumbfounded that the nurse had said that phrase in the year 1999. It could be demanding to care for him at times, but Connor couldn't imagine life without his Captain. Connor pushed the door the rest of the way open. "Okay, my handsome guy, let's get ready for bed." Connor said. Captain didn't hesitate or complain. He told the friend he had been chatting with that he had to go, they said their goodnights and goodbyes, and he powered off his equipment. Captain connected his phone and other portable devices to their chargers collected his nighttime snacks and got ready for bed. Connor did the same. They lied in bed, had their snacks, and watched another one of their favorite shows.

As interesting as the show was to him, not unlike some people, Connor could no longer hold his weary eyes open, and found himself fighting sleep. He knew that both the practices of snacking before bed and watching TV before bed were a point of contention for many people, but it was his and Captain's thing and would be a tradition that would be hard to break. He finally lost the battle with his eyelids and drifted off. His dreams were abundant and strange on this night. At first, there were familiar images and faces that he had recognized from the current day. And then, there were random images of people and places that were unfamiliar and he did not understand the meanings, not that one can always make sense out of a dream. But the weirdest dream of all, if it was indeed a dream, came last. Although at first, he was somewhat frightened, he was soon made to feel at ease by the presence of his dead wife. It was as if the bedroom filled with fluffy clouds, until everything was covered, leaving only a small opening in the center of the room, above the bed. Connor sat up in the dream, piercing the clouds out into the openness that remained. Connor had begun to look around, and started to panic, when Alexis materialized on the opposite side of the cloud-covered room, right in front of him. She appeared to be floating with cloud-like swirls slowly moving around her. The slow swirls kept Connor from seeing a distinct outline of her form. She was literally an angel, with wings. She would softly move them from time to time, but they had nothing to do with the fact that she was floating. She evidently sensed or saw the concern in Connor's eyes. "He's okay. He's lying right next to you, safely sleeping on a cloud." she said softly, smiling. Connor reached over and down into the cloud cover next to him toward where Captain would be lying in the bed and found his son and rested his hand on Captain's chest, feeling the gentle rise and fall of his inhaling and exhaling. Connor was unsure if he had really, physically just felt of Captain, or it was a part of a dream.

Although Connor was 99% sure he was dreaming, he decided to go along with however it may lead him. "We've missed you, Alexis." Connor said softly, again, not knowing if he was really speaking or just dreaming that he was. He felt as if he was in control of himself, but he wasn't entirely sure. Dream or not, he wondered if he should wake Captain. "I know, Connor. I've missed the both of you, but I've been watching." she said softly. "Well, if you have, I'm sure you've been disappointed in me." said Connor. "Not at all, my love. I know you've both had a tough time with me leaving. Like I told you, I want you two to be happy and always look out for each other and put each other first." whispered the apparition. "You should never doubt that, Alexis. I had just briefly lost my way until Francis put me back on the right track." said Connor, softly. "I know, my love. I know you always want to protect him and keep him safe. But something I know to be true now, and I need you to remember, is that Captain is a lot stronger than you think. Let him be a part . . ." she tried to finish whispering her sentence as she floated closer to Connor, but her image and voice began to fade away. The clouds began to swirl and started to disappear. As the apparition was dimming and becoming almost transparent, her body floated down into the dispersing clouds and her face got closer and closer to Connor's and lined up with his. Connor closed his eyes, expecting a kiss from the apparition. The kiss was not as romantic as he had thought it would be. He opened his eyes and Captain was sitting up in bed and had begun to laugh. Captain had jokingly tongue-kissed his dad in order to him to wake him up. "Yuck!" Connor exclaimed, wiping his mouth and laughing. He grabbed his man-kid and rolled around on the bed, tickling him. Although Connor's memory of the experience was fading fast, he now knew exactly what he needed to do.

| 17 |

Chapter 17: Take Your Kid to Work DAYS

Connor knew that there was an actual day in the United States dedicated for parents to bring their progeny with them to their place of employment. Connor joked with himself that this wouldn't really be any different. He had a long talk with his son about coming to work with him tonight. No phones or electronics out. If you have to talk, do so in a whisper. If you have to pee, use the portable urinal. If you have to do something else, then don't. Captain was very excited to go with his dad on his "pwivet vestgator" stakeout, as he called it. Captain said he was more than willing to make the sacrifices of electronics and basically sit quietly, possibly all night long. Connor, was, however, afraid Captain was going to be bored to tears. They took some drinks and snacks with them to keep the munchies and thirst at bay.

After dark, Connor headed to the address provided to

him by his client at the appropriate time. As he approached, since he saw no traffic or pedestrians, he turned his headlights off before he coasted in on the rear street of the apartment building. Like clockwork, Connor noted that his client had left the apartment complex at exactly the time she had said she would. Connor asked Captain to hand him his laptop computer. Captain excitedly did so. Connor booted the machine up and made sure the screen brightness was barely visible. He began to set up his surveillance system. Afterward, Connor and Captain simply talked about some things that held Captain's interest as they sat and waited. It was about an hour when a vehicle approached and parked on the same back street they were parked on. They had actually driven right by Connor and Captain and then parked directly in front of them. Connor scooted down in his seat and told Captain to do the same thing. A few minutes after they had heard the car's door open and close, Connor peered over his dash to make sure no one was there. "Okay, Captain, you can sit back up." said Connor.

Connor had a specially modified laptop computer designed specifically for surveillance and it was extremely rugged for use out in the field. It had antennas for receiving an audio and video stream. Connor made the surveillance software application on his computer active. Currently, the camera showed a dark bedroom, only it was bright green from the camera's night vision ability. He started recording. After a few minutes, the light in the bedroom switched on, and everything brightened with vivid color. A man and woman walked into the room, smiling, talking, and laughing, and sat right on the end of the bed, with their faces perfectly exposed to the camera. He recognized the man from the photo his client had given him, but the woman was definitely not his client. They spoke for another minute, then began to kiss, passionately. Connor looked over at Captain, who had been watching the screen with him. "Okay, buddy, you've seen enough of this." said Connor, and Captain looked away. Connor rotated the laptop, so Captain could not see it even if he had looked over at it. The man and woman had soon removed their garments and then the man turned the lights off. Their moments of intimacy were still very clear, even as bright green. Once Connor was satisfied with the amount of incriminating footage he had captured, he stopped the recording and shut down his laptop. He handed the computer to Captain, who placed it in its protective bag. He texted his client confirming her husband's infidelity and that he had the evidence she needed. She said she would see him in the morning at 9:00 am.

"Son, you understand that what they were doing was wrong?" asked Connor. "They not married." said Captain. "Exactly, they are not married. This is going to make the man's wife cry." said Connor. Captain nodded in understanding. "You can let the seat back and take a nap if you want, I'm going to wait and see what time the woman leaves." said Connor. Captain let the seat back and did as his dad suggested. They did not have to wait longer than another hour before the woman appeared once again, coming from the back of the apartment building. Connor scrunched down and waited until she had left. He sat back up and started the car. "Okay, Captain. You can sit up now if you want. We're headed home." said Connor. Captain did not respond.

Connor remained quiet momentarily and listened. He guiltily heard the soft snoring from his son. *Am I doing the right thing?* Connor asked himself. He turned his headlights back on and shifted the car into drive and headed home. It wasn't very late, but Captain said he was ready for bed. They followed their routine and went to bed. Before Captain went back to sleep, Connor asked him a question. "Son, did you like going with Daddy to work today?" Captain did not hesitate. "Yeah, I like to take down the bad guys! I go to work with you again?" Captain asked. "Is that what you want? To go back to work with Dad?" Connor asked. "Yes, Matey!" exclaimed Captain, excitedly. That dispelled a lot of the guilt Connor had been harboring for not only having his son out late but having him on a stakeout. Captain had stayed up much later than that before on his own. Although much of Connor's dream of Alexis was now lost to him, he could still clearly remember her saying *Captain is a lot stronger than you think.* He felt as if it was a sign of some kind. And she had mentioned something about letting him be a part of something. Be a part of his life? He always would be. Be a part of life in general? Be a part of his work? All of the above? Everything had gone so smoothly tonight, he definitely planned for Captain to go with him again. As long as there was no real danger, he didn't see what it could hurt. "You got it, Captain Kid!" Connor exclaimed, hugging and kissing his son. The two Gellars went to bed.

The following morning, the two Gellar men rose early, with bells on. At least, one of them did. "Come on, Captain, get up!" Connor exclaimed, tickling his son. Captain pulled the cover over his head and pretended to snore loudly.

Connor snatched the blanket down to reveal the big smile on his bright-eyed man. Captain did one of his trademark vies for affection, and held his arms up and out for a hug, hands balled up in fists, while he gently shook his arms, as if motioning *Wheres my hug? Wheres my hug?* Connor was more than happy to oblige his son's request for a hug. He squeezed Captain, and said, "Good morning, my man!" Captain offered his hand and Connor pulled him up. "Let's get ready for work!" exclaimed Connor. The two conducted their morning routines as quickly as possible and prepared for the day ahead.

Captain brought his phone, some custom coloring pages that Connor had made him, and a set of markers in case the day got too boring for him. Connor cleared off one of the end tables next to a chair in the corner of his office in order for Captain to have a place for his things and have room to color. He then began preparing a packet for his client who would be there in about an hour. He printed out the necessary documents, such as the report, the bill, a single explicit photo that he had snapped from the video, and placed them, along with a thumb drive of the actual video into a brown folder that closed with a clasp. He then began working on odds and ends of notes and research from other cases until his client arrived.

His office door opened, and Connor looked up to see Mrs. Stanton. *Soon to be Ms. Somebody.* Connor thought, a little sadly. "Hello, Mrs. Stanton. I hope you are well today, but I am sorry that we have to meet under these circumstances." said Connor. It was good for business, but he still felt bad that he was having to use that sentence or a variation of it so often when he met with such clients. "Hello, Mr. Gellar. I am doing okay, considering. I hope you are doing well." she said as she noticed Captain sitting in the corner, coloring one of his pages. Connor saw her glance at Captain. "I am well, thank you. Uh, that's my son, Captain. His daytime caregiver had a family matter suddenly come up. Do you want privacy?" Connor asked. The statement had actually been the truth, so Connor felt good about himself and what he had told her. "No, no, that's alright. Hello, Captain. It's nice to meet you." she said. Captain looked up from his coloring page, and stood up. He walked over to Mrs. Stanton and offered her a hug. She smiled and hugged him. "Meet you." Captain said. "You don't know how much I needed that hug." she said, smiling. Connor was relieved by Mrs. Stanton's attitude. Captain went back to his seat and continued coloring. "He's a sweet, young man." Mrs. Stanton said to Connor. "Thank you." Connor said.

Mrs. Stanton held her closed hand out over Connor's desk, palm down, obviously holding something and expecting Connor to retrieve it. He looked at her questioningly. She rotated her arm so that her palm faced upwards, then opened her hand, revealing the tiny camera she was holding. "Oh, yes, I'm sorry, I totally forgot. Thank you." said Connor. He retrieved the camera from her hand and stuck it into one of his desk drawers. He then retrieved the packet from his desk that he had prepared for her earlier and opened it. He pulled the explicit photo from the package and placed it face down on his desk, but left his hand on it. "The video is on a thumb drive in the package." said Connor. He made sure Mrs. Stanton had eye contact with him, then cut his eyes over to Captain. She glanced at Captain who appeared to be in his own world, coloring. She nodded in understanding, and pulled the photo up, making sure that Captain would not be able to see it from where he was sitting. When she laid eyes on the photo, they widened, and she nodded her head slowly with a look of disappointment on her face. "I knew it was her. I knew it." she said, bitterly. "So, I don't need to identify the female?" Connor asked. "No, I know the . . ." she began and looked over at Captain. "I know who she is." she said. Out of the blue, Captain decided to say "They aren't very nice to make you cry." Connor and Mrs. Stanton froze, and Connor blushed. "Captain, we don't need to talk about that." Connor said, firmly. "I'm very sorry, Mrs. Stanton, he must've over-heard me discussing this case with an associate – completely confidentially, I assure you – and drew his own conclusions." Connor said in a slight panic. Mrs. Stanton could see the concern on Connor's face. "Mr. Gellar, it's okay, really. Think nothing of it. Your son is absolutely right." said Mrs. Stanton, in a calming voice. Connor didn't feel so good about his statement this time, as it was a bald-faced lie. That's all he needed was for word to get around that he had taken Captain on a stakeout. "Mr. Gellar?" Mrs. Stanton asked. Connor's eyes had glazed over and his face was still flush. "Yes, I'm sorry, I'm still amazed at how much he understands." said Connor. "Please, relax. It's no big deal. How much do I owe you?" asked Mrs. Stanton. Connor pulled the bill from her package and quoted her the balance. "I'll be glad to give you a discount." Connor said, still a little flustered. Mrs. Stanton shook her head and said "Don't be ridiculous." She opened her purse and retrieved her checkbook. She wrote Connor a check. She had written it for $100 more than the balance he had quoted her. Connor offered the check back to her. "You've made a mistake, Mrs. Stanton, this is too much." he said. "That's no mistake, that's for doing such an efficient and professional job." she said. "Thank you, Mrs. Stanton. Thank you very much." Connor said. He wrote her a receipt from his receipt pad, placed all of her documents back into the package, and handed it to her. They shook hands. "Thanks again." he said. "Thank *you*." she said. She walked over to Captain, who looked up. She bent down and gave him a hug. "Thank you, too, Captain." she said. "You're welcome. 'Bye!" said Captain. "'Bye." she said. Mrs. Stanton left the office.

Connor had thought about whether to talk to Captain about his interactions with clients or just let it go. *Captain is probably the reason she gave us a tip.* Connor thought. He decided not to say anything. Like Mrs. Stanton had said, he had only been telling the truth, anyway. "You doing okay over there, buddy?" Connor asked his son. "Yep." Captain said, not even looking up. He had moved on from coloring to watching media on his cellphone. "Alright, Partner. Let Daddy get a little more work done, and then we'll see about finding something to eat, okay?" asked Connor. Captain looked up at Connor and licked his lips. They smiled at each other and then Captain went back to watching his phone. Connor began working on some administrative tasks for various cases. Connor's phone often went off with notifications of many kinds throughout the day. It was about 11 o'clock when he received "Making any headway?" from Daniel's burner phone. "Oh, no!" Connor said and placed his hand on his head. Captain looked over at his dad and said "What's wrong, Matey?" Connor slid his hand from his head to the back of his neck and rubbed it. "Nothing, Captain. I had just forgotten I was supposed to be helping Daniel." Connor said. "Daniel is coming to our house?" Captain asked, with his eyebrows raised. "No, not right now. Maybe he will another time." said Connor. Captain just nodded. Although they had already somewhat hashed things out, Connor still felt a little anger creeping in over the situation with Daniel. He remembered telling Daniel that Alexis was his friend, too, but he didn't even mention the fact that Captain thought the world of him. "Not yet, but I am working on it." Connor texted back to Daniel's burner phone. Connor was a good man, but no saint by a long shot. *By my count, that's two lies I've told and the day isn't over yet.* He thought. "What's for lunch today, Captain?" Connor asked. "Mexican!" exclaimed Captain. The two Gellar men locked up the office and headed for the local Mexican restaurant.

Mexican food was Captain's favorite. Most everyone at the restaurant knew him and showed him kindness there. He even had a special order that the cooks knew. It was called *Captain's plate.* The two men had a great time. It had been a while since they had just concentrated on eating something they liked and having fun doing so. After making a mental note to work on Daniel's case when they returned to the office, Connor told himself he was going to think of nothing else but Captain's happiness during lunch. While Alexis had been alive, whenever there would be occasions when only he and Captain would be eating or entertaining themselves for the evening, for whatever reason, they referred to it as *Two Boys Night.* Those were special memories. Only that's how it seemed it would always be from now on. When they had finished up, they stood up to prepare for their trip to the cashier. Connor was not a believer in coincidence, but as he was laying the tip down on the table, he spotted Daniel and Rachel enter the restaurant. He quickly told Captain to sit back down and not to move. Captain saw the look in his dad's eye and knew to do what he was told. Connor was in the perfect position to see the two detectives and not be seen himself if he just leaned to the right if they happened to look his way. Now, as long as they were seated in the back and not the front, he would be spared an awkward conversation. Even at a distance, he could see the light had left Daniel's eyes. He was basically a puppet. She was using his mistake to blackmail and control him. Connor didn't excuse Daniel's behavior or handling of the situation, but he also knew two wrongs didn't make a right. He was relieved when the hostess had them follow her to the back. "Let's go." Connor said quickly to Captain. They hurried to the cashier and Connor paid the bill.

Once they had returned to his office, Captain sat in the spot he had grown accustomed to, and Connor booted up his computer. After a substantial amount of time, he was able to pull up some information on the Harris family and found that the parents had been killed in an automobile accident. There had been some things going on in her life from then up until she had reached the age of 18, as he had found her records, but they were sealed by the NC age of majority law. His available legal resources were not able to find out the contents of the file. He did find several drug charges and assault cases that had been filed against her that had happened just after the age of 18, but strangely, all of the charges had been dropped. Another oddity was that there was absolutely no further activity after the age of 18. Although we all have some skeletons in our closets, the deeper Connor dug, it seemed her closet started out to be just a little fuller than most. But everything that she seemed to have been involved with, she eventually had somehow walked away squeaky clean. Otherwise, she probably would have never made it onto the force. Connor had friends that could probably get him access to Rachel's juvenile records, but the last thing he wanted to do was break the law. He could, however, possibly track down Rachel's first foster home or where she lived with family, and go from there. He continued to research all the information he could access, and worked into the evening, collecting data. It wasn't until Captain broke his concentration by saying "Matey, my belly is growling." Connor looked at his phone. "Goodness, Captain, I didn't realize it was getting so late, I'm sorry. Let's head home and we'll make some supper." said Connor. Carrying a small stack of printouts, Connor locked up the office, and they headed home.

Connor prepared one of their primary staples that Alexis had made them many times before, consisting of livermush, eggs, and grits. It was pretty fast and easy. Before bedtime, Connor continued to do a little more research on Rachel from his home office. Although he was unable to find any foster parent names, he was able to find the area where Rachel's parents were killed 14 years ago. Rachel was indeed an only child. Her parents were Todd and Elizabeth Harris. He printed out the remainder of the research he had collected and then powered down his computer. He headed to Captain's mancave to get him ready for bed. The room light was off. Connor switched it on and saw that Captain was not in the room. Since they had an alarm system, Connor no longer panicked when he couldn't immediately locate his son. He found Captain curled up on the loveseat in the living room where his mother had spent a lot of time. Sometimes when she had wished to stay up late to watch a TV show, she would go to the living room so as not to disturb anyone. As it was dark, Connor switched on the end table lamp. Captain had fallen asleep with a picture of his mother in his hand. He could see where his eyes were stained from tears. It hurt Connor's heart to think that he had been in here crying alone. Connor gently woke him. When Captain opened his eyes and saw his dad, fresh tears began to slide down his face. "I miss Mommy." he said. Connor hugged his son tightly. His son's tears caused them to spill down his own face as well. "I know you do, son. I miss her too. But you know, Mommy wants you to always remember her, but she doesn't want you to be sad." said Connor. The two men held each other for a while. When Connor felt that Captain had regained his composure, he and Captain performed their bedtime routine, and then went to bed.

"We've got a big day ahead of us, buddy." Connor said as he pulled out of the driveway. "Go where?" asked Captain.

"We're going to Garrington. We're going to see where a woman named Rachel used to live when she was a little girl." said Connor. He explained what he knew to Captain the best he could in a way he hoped Captain could understand. "Her mommy and daddy were killed in a car accident. Will you put the address in the GPS?" asked Connor, handing Captain his cellphone and telling him the address to put in. "Yep." answered Captain. "Spell it." Captain added. Sometimes Captain would use text-to-speech, but he would get frustrated when the technology could not understand him. Connor spelled out the exact address for Captain. "Got it!" he exclaimed. The phone was tied into the car via a cable, and the map on the car's view screen displayed the directions. Garrington was about two hours away. "Thank you, partner." said Connor as he ruffled his son's hair. They proceeded to the interstate and motored on to their destination. Captain provided the music from the media on his cellphone. Connor liked most of the music Captain listened to and was particularly happy when he found that they shared a liking for some music that was even older than Captain. Sometimes older than both of them put together.

The drive to Garrington had thankfully been uneventful. Connor found himself driving through an area that was commonly referred to as a *mill village* in Edmonton. The mill that had once been the employment-producing center of the village had long been shut down. There were various old structures, some made of red brick, that still remained and were enclosed behind a tall, chain-link fence with concertina wire at the top that ran the length of the entire fence as if it was a prison. The grass inside of the fence, along with other native vegetation, had reached waist-high lengths. Connor had memories of briefly living in an area such as this when he was a child. Captain had seen some similar areas as this before, but Connor could still see the fascination it held for him, as he turned his head to watch the old, mysterious buildings go by. "What are you thinking about, Captain?" Connor had to ask. "There might be dinosaurs back there!" exclaimed Captain. "I wouldn't be a bit surprised." said Connor, as he turned at the next street. He then pulled in front of the house that the GPS had indicated.

The tiny house was not quite a shanty, but not much more. Connor put the car in park but left it running. "Lock the door, I'll be back in a minute." said Connor, although the curb to the front door was only about twenty-five feet apart. After he closed the door, Captain hit the lock button. The lawn of the house wasn't nearly as tall as the mill property they had passed, but it was quite evident it had not been maintained in a while. The stepping stones that led to the front door were barely visible. He walked to the front door, climbed the few, rickety steps to the small stoop, and knocked on the door. After a couple of minutes with no response, he knocked again. "Ain't nobody lived there in years." a gruff voice said from nearby, startling Connor. They had not seen a living soul since they had entered the mill village, although there were random cars parked at some of the houses here and there. Connor looked around and found the source of the voice. An elderly man had come out of the house directly to Connor's left, as facing the house, and stood on his own stoop. Connor went back down the steps and walked from the yard he was in over to the yard of the man that was talking. "Hello, there, Sir." Connor said, politely, but still kept a respectful distance between himself and the man. The man was bald, with the exception of a few, thin swaths of hair on the sides. He had a slight hunch and was wearing a robe. Connor thought that he appeared to be in his eighties. The stoop of the man's house was slightly larger than the one Connor had left. It had some substandard two-by-four rails around it. The man did not respond to Connor's greeting, but laid his arms on one of the rails, leaning on it, as he faced Connor. After a few moments of silence, Connor asked "Do you know who owns the house?" The man's expression-less face did not change. "Nope." he said. "Did you know the previous residents?" Connor asked. "Nope." said the man. "Did you know *any* of the people that have lived here?" asked Connor. "I pretty much keep to myself." said the man, pronouncing *myself* as *muhself.*

Connor was exasperated. *If you keep to yourself, what are you doing out of your house, talking to me?* Connor thought, with irritation. "Well, thank you for your time, Sir." said Connor, as he turned to go back to his car. "Yep." said the man, holding his position, leaning onto his stoop railing. The window of Connor's sedan lowered and Captain stuck his head out of it. "This Rachel's house?" he questioned in a shout. Connor was preparing to tell his son that he didn't know when the old man said "Wait. Did he say *Rachel?*" Connor stopped dead in his tracks and turned back toward the old man. "Yes, Rachel. Rachel Harris. Did you know her?" asked Connor, as he walked back to where he had been originally standing, closer to the old man. Captain got out of the car and walked over to stand next to his dad. "Maybe. Why you askin' about Rachel, anyways?" the old man asked, lowering his eyebrows. "Well, it seems that she's in some trouble and I'm trying to help her." said Connor. *That could actually be partly true, so I'm still only at Lie #2,* Connor thought. "I haven't seen Rachel since she was a child. She's got to be up there close to thirty now? What kind of trouble is she in?" asked the old man. "Rachel is 26 now. Well, uh, she . . . it's very personal and has something to do with her growing up. I'm trying to find her foster parents." said Connor. *Yes! I could still be holding at Lie #2!* Connor thought, forcing himself not to smile. The old man was quiet for a moment. "Well . . . after Todd and Liz were killed, a couple that knew 'em pretty good stepped in. Of course, little Rachel was really sad about *both* her daddy *and* mommy gettin' killed, but after her precious *Moocheen* was gone, I didn't know if the girl was gonna make it or not." said the old man. "Who *Moocheen?*" Captain asked, puzzled. Connor looked at Captain, and raised his eyebrows, pleased with his son's insight. "You see, Liz – Elizabeth, and that probably weren't even her real name - came from China. Liz and Rachel had nicknames for each other. *Moocheen* was Rachel's nickname for her mother. Liz called Rachel *New-arr.* She was definitely a momma's girl. She followed Liz around like a puppy dog. It was real sweet to watch those two together. I have to say, that was the kindest family you would ever hope to meet." said the old man. "She call her mommy

Moocheen like I call you Matey. She mommy's girl like I daddy's boy!" said Captain, with an understanding of the old man's explanation. "That's right, my mister smarty pants!" said Connor, turning to his son and putting his hand on his shoulder. Captain smiled with pride. Connor wasn't sure, but when he looked back up, he thought he saw that the old man was on the verge of smiling. *Old Man-a-Lisa.* Connor thought, comically.

"So, then what happened?" asked Connor. "Well, that couple took Rachel to raise her, I reckon'. Todd had no family to speak of and Liz, being from China, nobody knew whether she had any family or not. 'Round here, 'specially back then, there weren't none of them social workers and such that really came 'round to these parts. We usually took care of things ourselves if we could. That couple that knew them was the Petersons . . . or, the Pattersons . . . it's hard to re-member. I didn't really know 'em, I just knew that Todd and Liz did." said the old man. "Do you know where they live?" asked Connor. "Well, they moved away not long after gettin' Rachel. They had just lived two or three streets over from us, that away." said the old man, pointing across the road in front of his house. "Do you think there is anyone else that may be able to tell us anything about that couple?" asked Connor. "I doubt it, there ain't many left around here. Y'all are lucky to have found me." said the old man. Connor nodded. "You've been a very big help, Sir, thank you so much for sharing what you know." said Connor. "Yep. Hope you're able to help that gal. I can only guess how hard it can be on ya to lose your parents when you're so young." he said. "My mommy pass away." Captain volunteered to the old man. "She did? I'm sorry 'bout that young man, but I bet she's in heaven right now lookin' down on you." said the old man. "She's my angel." said Captain. "I guarantee she is." said the old man, raising his hand in farewell. The Gellar men both waved at the old man, and then headed back to the car. When they got in, Connor clapped Captain on the back. "You're batting a thousand, Captain. You got us our next lead, my little investigator!" he exclaimed. Captain again gave him a big grin. Connor could probably use the town's online register of deeds to look for the information he needed. He wasn't going to fire up his laptop here. The old man made it clear that he keeps to himself, and yet, he was *still* on the porch, leaning on the rail, watching them. He was 99% sure the old man wouldn't care for them to stay parked there a while longer, but he shifted to drive and moved on until he found what looked to be a safe place to pull over and use his computer.

Captain handed Connor the laptop. He used the hotspot feature on his phone to provide a wireless internet connection. He did a search and quickly found Garrington's online register of deeds. After viewing some maps, plats, and deeds, he found the parcels of land in the area where the old man had indicated the couple that had taken Rachel had lived. Fortunately, they had not been renters, and following the chain of titles finally got him to an Otis and Cindy Peterson. The date on the transfer of ownership of the parcel matched the year that Rachel's parents had been killed, so there was little doubt to Connor that these were the right people. Through the use of some of Connor's other programs, resources, and the internet, after a short duration of research, he had located the current address of the Petersons. According to his information, they lived in another small town that Connor was also familiar with. He jotted down the address on one of the papers he had brought with them. He closed his computer and handed it back to Captain, who placed it back in its protective carrying case. "Go where, now, Matey?" Captain asked. Connor handed Captain his cellphone. "We are going to Torrenceville, North Carolina." said Connor as he began spouting out the address from his sheet. "829 West Pine Street, Torrenceville, North Carolina." said Connor. "Too fast, Matey!" exclaimed Captain. "Sorry, Captain." said Connor. He handed Captain the sheet and pointed to the address. Captain had known how to spell everything except *Torrenceville*. Captain punched in the address. Connor shifted into drive, and the two men headed to their destination.

Torrenceville was a small, but a bustling little country town which was only about an hour from Edmonton, their own home town. He was glad that it at least took them closer toward home. It was getting close to lunchtime, so Connor beat Captain to the punch, and asked "You ready to eat, big guy?" Captain nodded. "What would you like?" Connor asked. "How 'bout Meatloaf?" Captain asked. "Let's see what we can find." said Connor. They were cruising through the center of town when they saw one of the local mom-and-pop's greasy spoons right on main street. Connor swung into one of the vacant slots in front of the restaurant. He locked the vehicle and they went inside. The female server closest to them greeted them and told them to sit wherever they pleased. The place was pretty packed, but Captain found a booth next to the window. "I'll be with y'all shortly." said the server. The two Gellar men each picked up a menu and began perusing the restaurant's offerings. About the time Connor had spotted it, Captain eagerly exclaimed "They got country-style steak and gravy!" Connor smiled. "Country-style *snake?*" he asked, teasingly. Captain gave him a *behave yourself* look, lowered his eyebrows, and said "Country. Style. Steak." pronouncing each word carefully and with a pause between. "Oh, country-style *steak.*" Connor said, smiling, as if surprised. They both laughed at his silliness. The server came up to their table and asked "So, what would y'all like to drink?" Captain looked at his dad questioningly. Flavored, artificially sweetened, sparkling water was his Captain's usual beverage at home and usually got either a regular or diet soda when they went out. There was so much data back and forth about which was better for you, which was worse for your weight, and which would give you cancer, it made it hard for a parent to choose for their kid who absolutely would not drink plain water. "Get whatever you want, Captain." said Connor. Captain ordered a regular soda and Connor ordered plain water. "Do you know what you want to eat?" she asked. "Well, he does for sure. There are so many choices. Do you have a recommendation?" Connor asked. "Yes, go somewhere else." she whispered. Connor looked at her with surprise and then she immediately started laughing. "I'm just kiddin', sweetie, we have several restaurants in the area, and a few of them considered fancy, but *The Torrenceville Taste* has the best-tasting food in town!" the server exclaimed. "Whew, you got me."

said Connor. "Do you like chicken?" she asked. "Chicken is actually my favorite food." said Connor, smiling. "Well, then I have to recommend one of our local favorites. It's called the *Torrenceville Chicknado.* It's similar to a mini chicken pie if you've ever had one, only with our cook's special selection and combination of ingredients cooked in. I can honestly say it's very delicious." she said. "You sold me on that, I'll take one of those." said Connor. The server took down their food order. While they waited on their meals, they took the opportunity to go to the restroom and wash up.

While they were eating, when the server came by to check on them, she began to make idle chit-chat with them. "So, I haven't seen you two around here before. It's a small town and I know everyone. My name's Annie." she said. Annie was a very attractive southern woman. She had short, blonde hair, that appeared to be styled, only it was covered by the matching hat of her server uniform. She wore just enough makeup to enhance her appealing features, and not cover them up. She looked to be around Connor's age. Her body's inflection points were very favorable for Connor's preference, and guiltily, he knew that her overall appearance certainly had not hurt his eyes any. "Hi, Annie, I'm Connor, and this is my son. Everyone calls him *Captain.*" he said. "Nice to meet y'all" said Annie. Connor smiled and nodded. "Nice to meet you." said Captain. "You are just too precious!" exclaimed Annie with a smile, directing her comment to Captain. He returned her smile. Captain and Connor said "Thank you." at the same time. Annie chuckled and said, "You're not so bad, either." Connor could feel the heat of his face blushing. "Ditto for you, Annie." said Connor, still red. "Careful, Captain might tell Mrs. Connor." said Annie. "I'm afraid . . ." began Connor. "My mommy pass away." interjected Captain, sullenly. "Oh, I'm sorry, sweetie." she said. Whether it was just for a tip, or just genuine hospitality, Connor always appreciated a server that made sure to include his son in the conversation. Some people were a little uncomfortable around people with special needs. Connor didn't really hold anything against them, as he could remember his own hesitations when he was younger before his own precious son came along. "Are y'all staying with us for a while or just passin' through our little town?" she asked. "Well, actually, we're here to see some old family friends that we haven't seen in a long time." said Connor. *Darn it, Lie #3! I didn't think I was going to have to lie anymore after leaving the police force.* he thought, a little comically. *Being a good cop is one of the most honorable professions there are, but we sure are allowed to do some lying. Is it okay to lie for a good cause?* Connor's mind asked of himself. "Who're you here to see, if you don't mind me asking?" she asked. "The Petersons. Do you happen to know them?" The server's eyebrows raised. Connor could actually feel a new tension in the room. "Which Petersons?" she asked. "Uh, the Otis and Cindy Peterson family." Connor said. He felt the tension peak and Annie said "Hmm, I'm afraid I don't know them. Here's your check." She dropped the paper check on their table and walked away. As Connor had felt about Annie's interaction with Captain, he had also felt as if she may have been flirting with him. He noticed she was not wearing a ring or any jewelry for that matter. He was not so naive to know that her excessive friendliness could have either been an attempt at securing a tip, it could be her ordinary personality, it could be her genuine hospitality, or she could have actually been flirting with him. However, once Otis and Cindy Peterson were mentioned, she didn't want anything else to do with them. Connor paid for their meal and still gave Annie a nice tip. She had been very nice and an excellent server all the way up to the mention of the Petersons. He had thought of inquiring about Annie's attitude change, but ultimately just let it go.

After lunch, they completed their trip, and pulled in front of an average size home, just on the edge of town. Connor thought about telling Captain to wait in the car again but then thought *Captain is able to get people to talk better than I can. A skill he definitely got from Alexis.* "Come on, Son." he said. Captain followed Connor up the sidewalk. Once they had reached the door, Connor knocked. After a couple of minutes, Connor was preparing to knock again, when the interior door slowly began to open, revealing a very old woman. Her hair resembled an unkempt bird nest. She was wearing a faded moo-moo with various stains on it, partially covered by a tattered robe. She seemed to be having difficulty pulling the door open with one hand while holding on to a cane with the other. There was a storm door still separating them, but the glass was in the raised position, making communication possible through the screen. Connor leaned back and checked the numbers that were on the front of the house. 829. "Mrs. Peterson?" he asked. "Yes?" she said, eyeing Connor and Captain timidly. The old man back in Garrington hadn't said anything about the Petersons being an older couple, and he had not really payed attention to that data field when he had been searching. So, this didn't necessarily mean they couldn't have been older, but as forthcoming as the man had ended up being, Connor thought that this would have been a detail he would have volunteered. There could also be an error in the data he had researched. This may not be the Petersons he was looking for. "Is there an Otis Peterson here?" asked Connor. "No." she said flatly. Connor was unsure but thought that she had flinched slightly when he had mentioned the name *Otis*. "Are you Cindy Peterson?" he asked. "No." she said, impatiently. Connor had a gut feeling that this woman knew something. There was little he could do if she didn't want to talk to him. "Rachel's mommy and daddy are dead. They killed in a car wreck." Captain suddenly volunteered. The old woman's flinch was unmistakable this time. She moved her gaze from Connor to Captain. Connor could see memories containing pain and anguish escaping from the old woman's face. Captain saw them, too, and thinking the memories might be related to Todd and Elizabeth Harris he said "I sorry they dead." Tears began to spill down her face, and although he could not have done anything through the storm door, Connor jerked when he saw her sway slightly. She kept her balance by holding the open interior door and repositioning her cane. "Mrs. Peterson, we could really use your help." said Connor.

The old woman lifted the latch that unlocked the storm door. She seemed to only have enough strength to push the door out a few inches, and hoarsely she said "Come in." Connor gripped the storm door and opened it up. "Thank you."

he said as he waited for the woman to give them room to step inside. She moved very slowly and led them to her living room. The house was a complete mess and had an unpleasant odor. He didn't judge the woman for this, as she was barely able to get around, and seemed to be all alone. She more than likely would not have let Connor in if it weren't for Captain being at his side. "You are welcome to something to drink, but you'll have to fetch it from the kitchen. I'm not sure if I'd make it there and back right now." she said. Connor glanced at Captain in time to see him lick his lips. When it came to the possible opportunity for a sweet beverage, Captain was always ready, regardless of the conditions or circumstances. Connor quickly shook his head at him discretely, while the old woman was walking away from them, toward the living room. "We're fine, thank you." Connor said. As the two men passed a group of photos on the wall, Captain stopped and pointed at one of them "Look, Matey, Daniel!" he exclaimed. Although Captain's vision had always been monitored and was supposedly normal, he had mistaken and misidentified people in photographs on more than one occasion. Connor looked at the picture on the wall. Captain was wrong, the man wasn't Daniel, but he definitely had a striking resemblance. "No, son, that's not Daniel, but he sure does look like him." said Connor. Out of breath, the woman sank down into one of those chairs with a built-in power lift. She had been watching and listening to the Gellar's conversation, but she did not say anything. The tiny motors whirred as they brought her to a comfortable seating position. "Please, have a seat." she said. Connor and Captain sat on the couch that was opposite the woman's chair. "So, how is it that I can help you?" she asked. Connor felt as if he needed to be very careful with his wording. He was trying his best not to surpass *Lie #3*, but he also didn't know anything about this woman. For all he knew, she may be Rachel's mother and they have stayed in contact with one another. "So, you are not Cindy Peterson?" asked Connor. "No, she was my daughter-in-law." Mrs. Peterson responded. That picture you boys were looking at is my son, Otis. *So, she is also a Mrs. Peterson.* Connor thought. Connor noticed that she had said "was" her daughter-in-law. "Has Cindy passed away?" asked Connor. "Don't know and don't care." she said. "When was the last time you saw her?" asked Connor. Out of respect for Captain, she looked over at him and then back at Connor. "He's a smart, young man. You can say whatever you need to say in front of him." said Connor.

"I don't know how much you already know, and as embarrassing as it is, there's no point in holdin' back the truth. After child services took Rachel and the police arrested Otis, Cindy started runnin' the streets. Men and drugs, if you know what I mean. They eventually arrested her, too, for her involvement. I heard even though she hadn't done anything directly to Rachel, they had proven that she had known what Otis was doing, and was present during some of his abuse. But all she got was community service, can you believe that?" she asked, rhetorically. "So is your son still in prison?" asked Connor. "No, he was killed in there not long after going in. That's been a very long time ago. So, what's this all got to do with Rachel, now? I treated that girl as if she was my own flesh and blood, but she had never said a word about what Otis was doing, and of course, I never suspected nothin'. I never saw that sweet little girl again after they took her. Been over about 10 years ago or so, I reckon." said Mrs. Peterson. "Well, Rachel is now involved with someone, and they could be getting themselves into a whole lot of trouble. I was trying to find out what had happened to her in order to help them." said Connor. Mrs. Peterson sat quietly for a few moments. "When they had gotten Rachel and moved here, I moved in with them to help out. Otis had all but insisted that they didn't need any help, but I wouldn't take *no* for an answer. I can't believe what my son done to that sweet little girl right here under my nose. He did it for a couple of *years.* Cindy swore to me that she didn't know what was going on and she begged me to believe her, but she knew . . . she knew. Of course, I had *wanted* to believe her, but I just couldn't. There was no way she couldn't have known. And they had said they had somehow proven she knew. I let her stay here up until she had started runnin' around, then I threw her out. I say *let her stay,* but she probably could have thrown *me* out, seeing as how this was her 'n' Otis' house. But she was so strung up, when I told her to leave, she did. Ain't seen her since. That weren't long after Otis was killed in prison." she said. Connor thanked Mrs. Peterson and Captain gave her a hug. Connor could tell that it had been a while since Mrs. Peterson had really had any meaningful social interactions or relationships. She had probably been ostracized and been an outcast since her son's arrest and conviction. Connor knew all too well from his experience as a police officer that the *sins of the father* idiom could transcend not only in both directions of a generation, but could also cross the boundaries of gender as well. He could tell how Captain's hug had warmed her heart.

As they pulled away from the house, Connor said "Well, Son, it's official. You are a better private investigator than your Daddy is." Captain beamed with pride. "Daddy is the best." Captain said. "No, *you* are the best!" exclaimed Connor. "Matey is best!" exclaimed Captain. "No, no, no, my big man is best!" exclaimed Connor. Their back-and-forth banter had gotten them both giggling. As Connor was driving down main street, Captain waved at the restaurant they were passing and said "'Bye, Annie." Connor, who was driving very slowly through town, checked his rearview mirror to make sure no one was behind him, then slowed to a stop. He shifted into reverse, backed the car up the short distance back to the restaurant, and then pulled into a vacant parking spot. "Let's go." he told Captain. "Suppertime?" Captain asked. Connor smiled "No, not yet, buddy. I want to talk to Annie one more time." he said. They got out and went into the restaurant.

Annie looked up and saw it was them and said to the other server "You've got customers, Krystal." Connor could tell from Krystal's expression that she was not very pleased about her senior server sticking her with the two of them. Krystal stopped what she was doing and started walking toward the men. Connor held up his hand and nodded to indicate he did not need her. She rolled her eyes and went back to wiping the counter. Connor and Captain walked up to Annie. "Back so soon?" she asked with a plain and unfriendly voice and demeanor. She was rolling silverware and pretending to be too busy to even look at him. "Look, Annie, I just wanted to tell you that I'm sorry that I lied to you." said Connor. She looked up, without saying a word. Her facial expression was impatient and implied *Well, what do you want now?* "I didn't really know the Petersons. We are here because Rachel Harris and the man she is involved with are heading into big trouble. We're trying to find out what happened to her when she was a child, so we can help them both. Is there anything *you* can tell us that may be able to help." said Connor. Annie looked at Connor for several moments and then at Captain, who smiled at her. "Well, I do happen to know quite a bit. I'm only going to tell you because of this sweet guy, here." she said, referring to Captain.

Not only did she have them sit at a booth to talk, she gave Connor some coffee and a slice of pie, and Captain a small milkshake on the house. "Are you a cop or something?" Annie asked. "I used to be. Now, I'm a PI." said Connor. "Me, too. I'm a PI, too." said Captain. "Yes, Captain, you are the *best* PI. He really has been helping me tremendously. He's gotten more people to talk than I have." said Connor. "Including me. So, being a big cheese PI, you aren't able to find out everything that has happened to Rachel?" asked Annie, being playfully flippant. "Ouch, that hurts coming from you. Or anybody, for that matter." said Connor with a chuckle. Annie smiled. "We are trying, aren't we boy?" asked Connor to Captain. Captain nodded without releasing the milkshake straw from his mouth. "Only, there are certain things you can't look at as a PI, such as a child's sealed records. I mean, truthfully, I probably *could* get into them, but so far, I have drawn the line of my immorality at lying and I have not yet crossed it into breaking the law." Connor said, half-joking. Annie smiled again. "Well, sealed records or not, in a town this size, you are eventually going to find out every single little thing that happens to anyone in it." she said. "Lucky for me, then." said Connor. He filled Annie in with everything he had learned from Mrs. Peterson. She picked the story up from there.

"When Child Protective Services took Rachel on the day that they arrested Otis, she was 14 years old. Otis had been abusing her for 2 years! Some believe that Cindy was also involved, but supposedly all of the evidence to do with her was circumstantial. But, as Mrs. Peterson told you, she did get community service." Annie said. "They had found a foster home almost immediately. They could find no relatives, of course, and the couple they had placed Rachel with was the wealthiest couple in Torrenceville. So, you can only imagine how there was a lot of bending-over-backward to accommodate them. Once Rachel had been placed with them, the mother, Erica Duffield, immediately fell in love with her. Unfortunately, so did Bentley Duffield, only it wasn't the love you would be hoping for from a foster parent. Being the wealthy, fine, and upstanding citizens they were, it was no problem for them to go from foster parents to adoptive parents in no time at all. It wasn't out of the goodness of their hearts, either. At least, not out of his. Everybody knew they had been trying to have a baby for years with no success. It was rumored that they had actually spent a small fortune trying to have a baby of their own. Rachel, the poor thing, endured 4 more years of abuse until she was 18. She might would have been able to have gotten out of it before then if she had tried, but keep in mind, even as terrible as the circumstances were, this was her first stable home since her parent's deaths, and on top of it, she was living like a princess now. Being so young, she surely didn't know what would happen if she told anyone what was going on. And who knows, she may have chosen not to try to do anything about the abuse for fear of losing the one person who did care about her now, Erica. Not to mention her home with that lavish lifestyle. She was too young to know what she was doing. I'm sure she also knew that her adoptive father, Bentley was very influential. There's no telling what he may have told her to keep her quiet and try to keep control of her." said Annie.

"That's messed up." said Connor. "Well, it gets even messier. Rachel, of course wanted out of the abuse, but, as I said, maybe she didn't want to really leave her home, either. Maybe at one time, she thought things would get better as she got older. But after enduring it for 4 years, she had finally had enough. She also knew that she was of legal age to leave on her own. I'm sure she felt that she was owed something and wasn't going to leave empty-handed. Bentley had threatened that she wouldn't get a penny if she ever left. There was plenty of gossip and theories of what all Erica Duffield may have known to be going on, but if she had kept blinders on for 4 years, she certainly knew something was up when Rachel blackmailed Bentley for $100,000. She had said that if he didn't give her the money, in cash, she was going to the police and the newspapers. And she made sure to tell him "not just the local police" because she figured he might weasel his way out with them back then and that would get her nowhere." said Annie. "Did he pay her?" asked Connor. "Yes, he did. He didn't even hesitate, and it was rumored that he was very scared of her telling the secret. From what I heard, the Duffield's already had more money than they knew what to do with and they also had all these contracts doing some kind of business with the federal government. That was another rumor I picked up, instead of taking his *wife* out of town with him, he usually took Rachel when he went to some of these government facilities where they would stay overnight. And can you believe that's where he did a lot of the abuse? But he did also get her to agree to sign something that said she was no longer their daughter when he paid her off." said Annie. "An emancipation agreement." said Connor. "Yeah, that's it. Mrs. Duffield was torn up, of course, but from what I heard, she basically put up with him for the some of the same reasons Rachel did." said Annie. "Because it was their home and all they knew. Being wealthy sure didn't make it any easier. Is Erica still with him?" asked Connor. "No, she passed away not too long after Rachel had left. Of course, the whole town is suspicious of that, too, but when Bentley Duffield was out and about throwing his money around, most everyone seemed to conveniently forget what a snake in the grass he really is. He rarely comes into town since Rachel left. Darn near the whole police force and everyone on the city council have left and been replaced since all that had happened. But, as much as Mrs. Duffield loved her, she may have died from a broken heart when Rachel left." said Annie. "How is it that you know all of this?" asked Connor. "Like I said, it's a small town. Rachel was very seclusive, but she did have a few friends that were nothing but flatterers. You can't keep any secrets here. Unfortunately, rumors and hearsay don't mean a thing to the law. Not to mention, I have *my* own resources, *Mr. Detective.*" said Annie, playfully. "I'll bet you do." said Connor, laughing.

"So, how do *you* know Rachel?" asked Annie. "Rachel is also a detective. She's a police detective. She actually took my place when I was in a shooting incident that injured my leg, and so I left the force." said Connor. "You're kidding? On the one hand, after everything she's been through, it would make sense that she would want to be in a position to help people and see that justice is done, but on the other hand, while she lived here, most everyone said she dished out her own forms of abuse whenever she could. I think maybe her flatterer friends put up with it just because she would throw them a bone every now and then. Maybe money, expensive gifts, or even hand-me-downs. I figure that Rachel had lived life the way she had learned to live it. I had seen her before around town but had never really met her. None of the Duffield's came in *here,* of course." said Annie, pausing. "But that was almost 10 years ago. I believe people *can* change." she finished.

"Speaking of change, I wonder if the emancipation agreement was part of her changing her last name from *Duffield,* or if she just went back to *Harris* because she wanted to?" asked Connor, rhetorically. "If I would have gone through what she had, I would have changed my name. The last rumor I heard was that she was on drugs and constantly stayed in some kind of trouble." said Annie. "Well, she had been in some trouble right after she turned 18 and left the Duffields, but she ended up cleaning up and going to college. She majored in criminal justice. I remember how young she was when she joined the force. I didn't really know her that well, but I thought it was pretty impressive. She was a police officer and was going to night school." said Connor, as he knew that as fact. Annie nodded slowly in confirmation. "I may ask Mr. Duffield some questions. Would you happen to know where I could find him?" asked Connor. "Absolutely. 100 Duffield Drive." she said. "Of course." Connor said, laughing. After a moment, Connor's mood softened to a little bit more somber, as he reflected on something. "I would also like to ask you a favor." he said. "What is that?" asked Annie. "Since you seem to know just about everything, I assume you know that Otis was killed in prison. Since Cindy had disappeared, Mrs. Peterson has been left with no family at all." said Connor. "Yes, I do know about them. I don't much care what happened to Otis or Cindy. I don't really care about Mrs. Peterson, either. I think that Otis and Cindy both deserved what they got. As far as I'm concerned, allowing the abuse to happen is just as guilty as doin' the abusin'." said Annie. "That may be so, and I'm not saying I don't agree with you about Otis and Cindy. But what about Mrs. Peterson? Since you already knew what had happened to Otis and Cindy when I had first asked you about the Petersons, I assume you knew that there was only Mrs. Peterson there, now, and you immediately seemed to show nothing but disdain for her." said Connor. "Well, she's the mother of a monster!" exclaimed Annie. "Do you really *know* Mrs. Peterson?" Connor asked. "Well, no, not personally." responded Annie. "Mrs. Peterson is very sweet." said Captain. "Yes, Annie, she *is* very sweet. I feel in my heart that she had nothing to do with any of the abuse and she didn't have a clue it had even been going on until Otis had been arrested. Although I'm not always right, I've always been a pretty good judge of character. I have been practicing that skill as part of my living for many years now. Unless I have missed my mark, I judge you to be the kind of person that wouldn't let a decrepit woman suffer and go uncared for without at least looking into it. She doesn't have any family, and I'm afraid if she doesn't get some help soon, she's going to end up dying alone." Connor said. Annie lowered her eyes from Connor's gaze. He reached out and put his hand on her shoulder and she slowly looked back up and stared into his eyes. He saw a tear slide down her cheek and he looked deep into her eyes and recognized a look that was all-to-familiar: shame. With his other hand, he touched her face and used his thumb to wipe away the tear. "It's not your fault, Annie. We all assume the worst of people that have a tie to someone who is guilty of doing bad things. It's nothing to be ashamed of." Connor said. "I feel terrible. I will go see her and see what I can do. I promise." said Annie. Connor gave Annie a hug. It was purely for support, but as he held this woman, he felt a sensation of longing and an electrifying feeling that he had not felt since Alexis. Guiltily, he almost pulled away, but then wondered what she would think if he broke the hug off so suddenly. When they finished their embrace, they both looked into each other's eyes. "You're a special man, Connor." said Annie. Connor wasn't sure, but he thought Annie might have felt the electrifying sensation as well. "You're a pretty special woman." he said. "This was a very special milkshake." said Captain. They all started laughing as Annie was rubbing away the fresh tears that had begun falling while she was embracing Connor. When the laughter had died down, Connor said "Well, Annie, I can't thank you enough for your real southern hospitality. I truly have enjoyed your company and wish we had time to stay longer, but I guess we need to head out." He stood up and clapped Captain on the back. Captain also stood up. "It was a pleasure talking to you two. I wish you both the best of luck. I hope y'all will come back to see me again." said Annie. She hugged Captain, and then gave Connor another hug. As she was hugging Connor, he again felt that familiar sensation of longing. It didn't help that she had whispered *I really do want to see you again* in his ear during the hug. "I'll come back; I promise." Connor whispered in her ear before he even realized that he was going to do so. Connor and Captain headed for the door, and then Connor stopped and turned back to Annie. "Can you do me *just one more* favor?" he asked, smiling. "Sure." said Annie. "I'd really rather that my investigation not be the talk of the town." he said. Annie smiled. "My lips are sealed." she said as she pursed them and held her index finger against them.

Connor spelled the road name for Captain and they headed for Duffield Drive. Their destination had them drive just outside of town, into some beautiful countryside. When they reached Duffield Drive, they saw a *Private Property / No Trespassing* sign at the beginning of the road. The sign was not a cheap, red and white plastic sign you could buy from any retail store. It was a larger, custom-made wood sign, with a green background and white lettering, so as not to be aesthetically inconsistent with the wooded surroundings. The private driveway was paved and did a great deal of winding up an incline, through a forest. It eventually came out at a beautiful manor that was perched on the top of a luscious green hill. The hill was in the middle of a large, gorgeous yard, surrounded by the forest. There was a closed, fancy, wrought-iron gate between two huge, decorative, brick pillars blocking further ingress. The gate was several hundred feet from the house, and wrought-iron fencing extended from each brick pillar into the woods that surrounded the property. Connor noticed that there were power gate-openers on each gate so that both gates could be opened remotely. He could also see two security cameras, one mounted on each brick pillar. There had been no attempt to mask the presence of the cameras. There was a black, steel post, a little taller than the height of an average car's window sill, in between two steel, white-painted bollards in the center of the driveway, standing about 30 feet in front of the gate. Connor pulled up to the post. There was a multi-purposed panel mounted on the top of the post. There was a numeric keypad, a contactless smart card reader area, and an intercom button, next to a microphone and speaker. Connor had not really thought about what he was going to say, but he went ahead and pressed the intercom button.

After a brief delay, a female voice came out of the small speaker. "Yes, can I help you?" the voice asked in a professional manner. Connor cleared his throat. "Uh, yes, is Mr. Duffield home?" Connor asked. After another brief delay, the voice returned. "I'm sorry, Mr. Duffield is not currently available. If you would like, I can take your contact information and see that he receives it." said the voice. Connor was not at all surprised at the brush-off. He remained quiet for a moment, thinking. "Okay, then. Could you please just let him know I was wanting to talk to him about Rachel." said Connor. There was a moment of silence, then a man's voice came out of the speaker. "Who is this and what do you want?" the voice asked. "Well, Mr. Duffield, I just wanted to ask you a few questions about Rachel." said Connor, taking a guess that the voice did, indeed, belong to Mr. Duffield. There was more silence. "You know, the Rachel Duffield that used to be your daughter. Remember?" asked Connor. "That's public knowledge." said the voice. "It's also pretty much public knowledge how she was abused for years and then someone paid her off to keep her mouth shut when she had finally gotten old enough to leave." said Connor. "Well, those are some very strong accusations. It's very possible that someone saying such things about *me* might find themselves in a slander or defamation of character lawsuit. What do you think of that, Mr. . . what did you say your name was?" said the voice. Connor was too experienced to have committed slander, and he had been very careful how he had worded his previous statement. There was always the possibility he was being recorded, either directly because of the conversation, or simply as a feature of the estate's fancy security system. "I didn't say." said Connor. "Well, in any case, I suggest you get off of my land before I have you arrested for trespassing." said Bentley Duffield. Connor knew the law better than most. Mr. Duffield indeed had every right to call the police, have them removed, and possibly even arrested. He had already committed second-degree trespassing just by driving up the driveway. The last thing he wanted to do was aggravate a man of such wealth and influence with nothing but hearsay evidence, especially when it was himself technically in the wrong. "I'm leaving." said Connor. "Of course, you are." said Duffield. Connor shifted the car into reverse and backed up until he felt as though the cameras on the brick pillars could not see his license plate when he turned around. Not that there couldn't have been other cameras that he had not seen, but at least he knew he was doing what he could to avoid being easily identified. He got the car turned around and headed back down the winding road. Connor handed Captain his cellphone. "Let's go home." Connor said. Captain typed "home" into the cell phone's map program, and the map popped up on the car's screen providing them with directions. As they traveled down the long driveway, Captain leaned over in his seat, toward Connor, and whispered something into Connor's ear. Connor nodded and said "Yes, that man is *definitely* one of those."

Chapter 18: Back to Business

Before they arrived home, since it was getting late, they swung by a fast-food restaurant and picked up something for supper. Chili and a baked potato for Captain, and a burger with fries for Connor. When they arrived home, there was a small package on their front porch. Captain went into the house and took their food to the kitchen and placed it on the counter so Connor could prepare it. Connor went out and retrieved the package from the porch. He opened it in the kitchen and surprised Captain with it. "Captain, if you're going to be my partner, you're going to need this!" exclaimed Connor, as he held up the object. It was a large magnifying glass, trimmed in solid brass. It was the kind of magnifier that Connor had seen depicted being used by investigators and detectives on the covers of some of Captain's books and movies. "No private investigator should be without one of these!"

Connor exclaimed, handing the magnifying glass to his son. Captain took the magnifier and squeezed his father tightly. "Thanks, Matey!" he exclaimed, excitedly. "You're welcome, son." said Connor. Captain immediately began peering at items around the kitchen, revealing details on various food products and appliances that were not readily visible to the naked eye. Connor smiled watching his son and began preparing their takeout.

They watched some TV together in the living room as they ate. Once they had finished, Connor told Captain he could play for a little bit, because he had some work to do. He wanted to take care of a few things before lying down for the night. He made notes of everywhere they had been, everyone's names that he had talked to or learned of, and all of the information he had collected throughout the day. He texted *Possible 5150,* the police code for mental health crisis, to Daniel's burner phone. He then put his phone on charge and made sure all of Captain's devices were charging as well. He then asked Captain to brush his teeth, shower, and get ready for bed. Connor did the same.

When he got up in the morning, he checked his cellphone. There were the usual texts, missed calls, and voicemails from current and prospective clients, but Daniel had also returned his text sometime in the night. It simply said *I already knew that. That's why I need help.* Connor went ahead and texted him back: *I wanted you to know that I'm working on it.* Connor woke Captain and they had their medicines, vitamins, and breakfast. They gathered the items they were taking with them, prepared for the day ahead, and then headed to the office.

Once in the office, Connor reviewed his schedule for the day. *I need to get some work done for some of my paying clients.* Connor thought. He felt bad about thinking it, but he couldn't help Daniel if he fell behind in his regular business. He had dedicated the entire day to Daniel's problem yesterday and apparently had only found out what Daniel already knew: Rachel probably had some mental issues. *Was the whole day wasted?* he questioned himself, with frustration. "Come on, Captain, let's get out of here." said Connor. Captain looked at him with surprise. "Go where?" Captain asked. "Let's go do a little stakeout." said Connor. Captain jumped up and followed his dad out of the office. Connor sat in the car for a few minutes, as he needed to make some calls. The stress of keeping up with business and evidently doing a bad job for Daniel was getting to him. His revenue stream was okay, but he couldn't do a good job for anyone if he didn't increase his productivity. Connor started the car and headed to the local furniture store.

He and Captain went inside and Connor led Captain to the recliner section. He found the brown ottoman he was looking for. One of the furniture store associates approached them. "Hi, can I help you find anything?" the man asked. "I believe we've found what we're looking for." he said, nodding at Captain who was sitting on the ottoman. The man raised his clipboard, and flipped through the sheets. "Okay, that's the russet-colored chair and ottoman set. It's on sale for $499." the man said. "I just need the ottoman." said Connor. "The basic ottoman is . . . uh, $99." said the associate, referring back to his sales sheet. "Can you tell me a little bit about the specifications, mostly, how much does it weigh?" asked Connor. The sales associate flipped back to the page and scanned the product description. "Yes, it weighs about fifty pounds." he said. "Can you deliver it today?" asked Connor. "Hold on, and let me check." said the associate. He walked to the sales counter and spoke to the woman behind the counter. He could see her look through a clipboard she had on the desk. The associate walked back to them. "We sure can. When would you like it delivered?" he asked. "Immediately." said Connor. "We can do that. You know there is a delivery fee, right?" asked the associate. "How much is it?" asked Connor. "Is the delivery local?" asked the associate. "Yes, very." replied Connor. "There will be $25 charge for local delivery. This item should fit in your car, if you'd prefer to take it from the store." said the associate. "That's okay. One more thing, do the guys help the customer carry the furniture into the home?" asked Connor. "If you want them to, they will bring it in and set it up." said the associate. "No, no, I actually don't want them inside of the house for personal reasons. I just want them to knock at the door, make sure someone answers, and leave it. Please make a note that no one is to enter the house. I'm giving this as a gift." said Connor. The sales associate was a bit confused about Connor's odd request but did as he asked. "Also, I'm going to need a bill of sale and a copy of that spec sheet." said Connor. "Yes, Sir. There will be a spec sheet included with the product." said the associate. "Okay, but do you mind making a copy for me. As I said, I'm giving it as a gift, and I need this for my records." said Connor. "Yes, Sir. If you'll just come over to the cashier, I'll have her ring you up while I get that copy for you." said the associate. Connor followed the associate to the register, and the cashier checked him out. "After tax and delivery, that comes to $130.93." she said. Connor gave her $140 and she counted out his change. The sales associate came out of the back with a copy of the product's specification sheet. "I need your address for the delivery, Sir." said the associate. Connor pulled out his phone looked through his notes. He gave the man the address, and then he and Captain left the store.

They parked on the street opposite the house with the address that Connor had provided to the furniture store. He asked Captain to get his camera ready. Captain pulled the large camera out of its custom bag, turned it on, and handed it to his dad. *It's a very bright day, so lighting shouldn't be a problem.* Connor thought. He twisted the lens of the DSLR camera and zoomed in and out at particular areas of the home and took some test pictures. They were sharp and clear. It was less than hour when the furniture store's delivery truck arrived. Connor, who had found himself under a lot of stress lately, had fallen asleep. If not for Captain shaking him and exclaiming "Daddy, truck is here!" he would have slept through the entire delivery. Connor groggily shook the sleep off and grabbed his camera out of his lap. He looked through the viewfinder and saw nothing but black. He remembered he had put the lens cap back on, as the lens costed more than the camera did. He popped it off and aimed in the direction of the house and delivery truck. "No, way!" he exclaimed. The delivery man had already unloaded the ottoman from the back of the truck, and he was parked between Connor and the subject's front door. Connor had to make a snap decision. He was most definitely going to miss the shot if he just sat there, but there was the chance of getting spotted if he either moved the car or got out, and he was pretty sure time was running out. He pulled on the car door handle to open it just as the delivery truck began pulling away. All he saw was the subject's front door closing. Connor laid his camera in his lap and put his hand to his forehead, and blew out of his mouth slowly, as he bowed down in the seat. He was exasperated. Captain reached over and hugged his dad. "I'm sorry, Daddy." Captain said. "It's not your fault, buddy. Daddy messed up." said Connor hugging him back. Captain stroked Connor's hair, as he could tell his dad was upset.

Connor had followed the subject for several days as part of a workman's comp case the week before Francis had been forced to stop taking Captain with her. The man had been very careful out in public. He wore his neck brace just as he was supposed to and did not offer to lift *anything,* let alone something over 25 pounds. The last place he had followed the subject was a trip that he had taken to the very furniture store that Connor had just purchased the ottoman from. The subject had his wife with him, and they got into an argument over which ottoman to purchase, and ended up not purchasing anything. They had been speaking with one of the sales associates, but the man had walked away when the couple chad begun arguing. Connor remembered the one that she had wanted, and that was the one he had purchased today. He was already on the fence as to whether or not the worker's comp representative would accept the $130.93 as an expense, but now he would definitely be out the money. He still couldn't believe he had made such a rookie mistake, and parked where the delivery van would block his line of sight to the subject's front door. *I've got to slow down. I'm trying to rush these jobs because I'm worried about my state of affairs.* Connor thought. He had again found himself dwelling on what he felt were constant misfortunes and was throwing himself a pity party when Captain exclaimed "Matey, look! The man!"

Captain had already known to pull away from his dad where he had been hugged up to him and give him some room. He handed Connor the camera. Connor leaned back from his bowing position. He pointed out the window and was holding the shutter button down before he had actually seen the man or even checked his zoom. As his pictures were snapping, Connor looked through the viewfinder, and twisted the telephoto lens. He could see the subject's face clearly, and he had his old ottoman over his shoulder and was carrying it out to the curb. The man actually had a huge smile on his face and was not wearing his neck brace. He had taken many good pictures of the man with the ottoman over his shoulder. He waited a few minutes after the man had gone back into his house, walked over to the curb, picked up the old ottoman, and placed it in his back seat. All he had to do now was photograph it while weighing it, write up his report, and prepare his package. He would keep the old ottoman around for the time being, just in case. "Son! You've done it again! You are the best private investigator in the world!" Connor exclaimed. Captain beamed with delight. Although he was the most loving person Connor knew, he was also a lot craftier than some people would believe, because he immediately took advantage of the situation and simply asked "Milkshake?"

Connor took Captain by his favorite fast-food place and got him a milkshake. Connor was by no means a fan of instrumental feeding, but Captain was the exception to the rule. Sure, he needed to shed a few pounds, just like most of us do, but he was healthy and did exercise with his dad from time to time. Although Connor and Alexis had tried to keep his life as fulfilled as possible, which Connor was still trying to do, they also knew that he might miss out on quite a few experiences that his typical peers would not. They certainly were not going to deny him some simple pleasures or frivolities every now and then. All parents are faced with situations of *give and take* with their children. Perhaps only parents of a person with special needs would understand these other unique, compromising challenges. Connor would continue to honor Alexis' memory and both of their hopes and dreams for Captain by allowing him to always live life to the fullest, learn as much as he could, be as happy as he can be, and learn to be as independent as possible. There was still time left for a little office work, but instead of going to the office, Connor headed home. He cut Captain loose to entertain himself while he took care of a few odds and ends. He photographed the old ottoman on his bathroom scale. It was much heavier than the new one, as it weighed almost 75 pounds. He texted his worker's comp client and asked if the man could come to the office in the morning. He confirmed that he could. Being in high spirits again, he thought about what he could do for

Daniel. He checked his phone. Daniel still had not responded to Connor's last text *I wanted you to know that I'm working on it.* Connor added another line to the text. He sent: *We need to meet again. I think we need to look in the home. Is there some way you can do that?* The two Gellars finally called it a night and went to bed.

The next morning, in the office, Connor and Captain would take turns yawning. When Connor saw Captain yawn, it would make him yawn, and vice-versa. As another "treat," he had let Captain stay up late. This, of course, meant he had stayed up late because he never went to sleep until Captain was safely in bed. He had always been called an overprotective parent by many and his response had always been the same, "I would rather be overprotective than under-protective." He would say it somewhat indignantly, but he knew that what they had said was probably right and that there had to be a happy medium in there somewhere. Connor just never could seem to find it. He had always been a worrier and had almost always erred on the side of caution. Captain had made a habit of carrying his magnifying glass with him. He was currently using it to see closeups of his coloring pages, the details on the sides of his markers, and other details of his surroundings, such as his chair, the lamp, and the table.

The client walked into the office just as Connor was placing the last of the items from the printer in the man's package. "Good morning, Mr. Barnes." Connor said. "Good morning." said Mr. Barnes. "That's my son, Captain. He's the one that nailed this case shut." said Connor. "Oh, really? Well, good morning, young man." said Mr. Barnes. "Mornin'." Captain said, yawning. "We had a late night last night." said Connor. Connor opened the package that he had just finished closing. He showed Mr. Barnes one of the best photographs that had the subject carrying the ottoman. He then showed him the one displaying the weight of the ottoman. "I have the actual ottoman just in case it's needed." Connor informed him. "Ahh, these should do nicely. Do you have the bill?" asked Mr. Barnes. Connor pulled it out of the package. Mr. Barnes scrutinized it. "Why is there a charge for a new ottoman on your itemized expenses?" asked Mr. Barnes. "I was having difficulty catching him in a compromising situation. In order to expedite the case, I baited him with a new ottoman and it worked. That's his old one he is pictured with." explained Connor. "I see." said Mr. Barnes, rubbing his chin. "What would you say to half of the cost of the ottoman, and we will pay the remainder if and when the case is won and closed?" asked Mr. Barnes. "I believe that would be more than fair." said Connor. "Excellent." said Mr. Barnes. He subtracted $65.47 from Connor's total bill and wrote him a check. As a courtesy, he also wrote a note of what they had discussed about paying Connor the remaining $65.47 at the close of the case and signed it. Connor wrote him out a receipt. They thanked each other and Mr. Barnes left. Connor began doing some administration work and research on some of his other cases.

He was transferring notes from the computer screen to his notepad when the door to his office opened and Daniel stepped in. Both of the Gellars looked up. "Daniel!" shouted Captain as he jumped up and ran to him. Captain gave Daniel a hug which Daniel returned. "Hey, buddy, how ya been?"

Daniel asked him. "Good." he said. Captain's demeanor almost immediately changed and his shoulders slumped slightly. "Mommy pass away." he said gloomily. "I know, Captain, I'm so sorry about that. I know you didn't see me, but I came to her funeral." said Daniel. "You there?" Captain asked. "Yes, I was there, but I had to keep it secret. You know that's how detectives are sometimes." said Daniel. Captain nodded and gave Daniel another hug. "I'm a pwivet vestgator, now." said Captain with pride. "You are?" asked Daniel. "Yeeepp." said Captain, dragging the word out. "I'm sure you're much better than your dad." Daniel said. "We make a great team." Captain said, bluntly. "I'm sure you do." said Daniel. "He actually has been an amazing help to me." said Connor. Daniel raised his eyebrows. "I believe it." Daniel said.

"Did you not get my texts?" asked Connor. "Yes, but Rachel was heading back to the car before I could respond, and I had to hide the phone again." explained Daniel. "Well, it looks like you're free enough now to respond and let me know something." Connor snapped. "Look, I'm sorry. It's hard keeping up with everything when you're living a secret life! I can't carry the phone on me, and I have very little time to myself! My wife is suspicious, so she is extra clingy. Rachel has been on my heels from day one, and getting as clingy as my wife is now, but she doesn't seem to care about the balancing act I'm having to perform! Even though this situation could end her career, too, she acts as if she isn't one bit worried about it. Every time I need to check that phone, I have to undo the clip from the seat cover and fish it out from where I had stuffed it down into the seat. Then, I have to wait forever for it to power on. Then, when I'm done using the tiny, cumbersome keypad, I have to switch it off, stuff it back in the seat and get the seat cover clip back in place. It's really nerve-racking when you wonder if you're going to get it done in time or if this will be the time you get caught." exclaimed Daniel with exasperation. Captain had seated himself back in his usual spot and was watching his dad and Daniel go back and forth. Connor looked over at Captain and could see the anxious look in his eyes as if he was expecting their fraught exchange to continue to worsen. Connor breathed in deeply and let the air out slowly. He relaxed and let calmness settle over him. After a few moments, when he felt as if his agitation had passed, he asked Daniel "So, what's the current situation?" Daniel reached into his pocket. "Well, you remember how I managed to slip away the last time? The same M.O. as before. Now, I've got these." Daniel said. He pulled his hand out of his pocket and dangled a set of keys in front of Connor. "Her house key?" Connor asked. "She *gave* me her apartment key and wanted me to invite you to see her place. But remember, we don't have a lot of time." said Daniel, phrasing his statements in such a way that technically there would be nothing incriminating tied to the Gellar men, which Connor immediately understood. "Let's go." said Connor.

"Let's take my car just in case I have to take off unexpectedly." said Daniel. "Good thinking." said Connor. They piled into Daniel's sedan. "What about Captain?" asked Daniel in a low voice, nodding toward the backseat as Captain fastened his seatbelt. Daniel was completely unaware of how Captain had been accompanying Connor since Francis had to stop caring for him. "Are you kidding me? He's the BEST partner

I've ever had!" exclaimed Connor. "Ouch, that really hurts." said Daniel as he started the car. He shifted the car into drive and began heading to the apartment building where Rachel resided. After they had been traveling for a few minutes in silence, Connor said "You know Daniel, I'll always be thankful for having had you as my partner and I'll always be grateful to you for saving my life." Daniel glanced over at Connor and then back at the road. "I know that, buddy. I will always be thankful that you were my partner. I know the day of the shooting; you'd done the same for me." said Daniel. "I would have, Daniel, without hesitation." said Connor, looking over at his friend. "You know, Connor, I used to have two partners like the one you have in the backseat. Seems like one day, we were having a shootout, using the box our new refrigerator had come in as a hideout, and then I blinked my eyes, and then they both had left for college and never came back." said Daniel forlornly. "Yeah, I can imagine how that can hurt, buddy. Even though my partner will hopefully be with me forever, you are also privy to some of the challenges that I've had with him that you haven't had, either. I know you wouldn't trade your experiences for anything in the world . . . and neither would I. As I said, I will forever be grateful to you for saving me, but the partner I have now may have saved my life a long time before you did." said Connor. "I know that, buddy. You've got a real special partner back there." said Daniel.

They pulled into the empty, designated space for Rachel's apartment. Daniel had been here with Rachel before, when she needed to come by to retrieve something, but she had never asked him inside. "Remember the last time, she was still asleep when I returned to her and she slept for a little while longer, but the effect may not always be the same. How 'bout we not take the scenic route." said Daniel. "Gotcha. You do realize if we get caught, we could be looking at jail time. I will lose my PI license, not to mention, I could lose Captain." said Connor, as he gripped the car door handle. Daniel looked over at Connor. "So, let's not get caught." he said. Connor let go of the door handle. "Really? That's what you've got?" Connor asked. "Look, we already know there are no security cameras here. I'm the one with the keys and as I've said, I'm inviting you in to see my mistress' place. I've told so many lies, I'm in so deep, and I'm probably already going to be in so much trouble now, I'll do or say whatever I have to in order to keep y'all out of this." said Daniel. They got out of the car and headed for the apartment.

Daniel quickly found the correct key, unlocked the door, and invited the Gellar men inside. Connor and Daniel immediately pulled nitrile gloves from their pockets and donned them. Connor had an extra pair for Captain and assisted him in putting them on. "Captain, listen to me buddy, don't touch *anything*. If you see something, just let me or Daniel know, okay?" asked Connor of Captain. "I not touch nothing." said Captain. Rachel kept her place pristine. It was only a modest, one-room apartment. It was clean enough to have passed an inspection from the toughest drill sergeant at boot camp. The decor, although it was very sparse, unsurprisingly to Connor, maintained a decorum of an Asian theme. All of the floors were hardwoods, and they were shiny and beautiful. He had a feeling Rachel had the floor done on her own, as it seemed to be worth more than the apartment itself. The three men split up and began looking around. Daniel headed deeper into the apartment, presumably toward the bedroom. Connor went into the kitchen. Captain began walking around in the living room.

Daniel quickly opened and closed all of her dresser drawers, careful not to disturb her clothing when he stuck his hand down into the bottom of each drawer to feel if anything was hidden. Connor quickly opened all of the kitchen cabinets and checked all of the food packages that might could hold something besides food, and carefully replaced them. Captain walked around the living room doing as he had been instructed: *not touching anything.* He was, however, examining everything through his magnifying glass. Unsuccessful with any of Rachel's drawers, Daniel looked under her bed and then in the closet. He finally found something of interest in a shoebox and went to get Connor to look in it with him. Connor had just finished looking through the stove and refrigerator, and then he joined Daniel in Rachel's bedroom. He carefully opened the lid and made a mental note as to how he removed the items from the box on the chance that Rachel might notice they had been disturbed. There were many trinkets and keepsakes that really did not seem to be of any help, but there were some old photos in the box, that if not helpful, were definitely interesting. There were a few very old pictures of some older couples. On the backs of the photos, the handwriting was evidently Chinese, as they were odd characters that looked familiar, such as the characters printed on some of the literature Connor could remember seeing on instruction booklets for products and such. He assumed that these older folks may have been Rachel's parents and grandparents. As they flipped through the photos, they finally came across an older, but more recent one. He could tell it was Rachel as a child and assumed she was with her mother and father. He flipped it over and it had the same type of characters on the back as all of the rest of the photos had. Connor pulled out his cellphone and took a picture of the front and the back of the photo. He and Daniel carefully replaced the contents of the shoebox as they had removed them, and then Daniel placed it back in the exact location and position it had been. "Daniel, we haven't nearly covered enough ground, but I'm afraid we're running out of time." said Connor. Daniel looked at his watch. "I'm afraid I agree with you. If we leave now, I should be back to the motel within about the same amount of time that had passed before." said Daniel. Daniel made sure everything in Rachel's bedroom was as he found it, and then they headed up the hallway.

When they had entered the living room, Connor saw Captain examining a small figurine of a Chinese woman wearing a kimono on one of the end tables, scrutinizing it through his magnifying glass. It was in front of other small, Chinese figurines. When Connor saw how close he was to the figurines, he was afraid he was going to bump them with his magnifying glass, and possibly knock them off of the table. "Captain!" Connor exclaimed as loudly as he dared. Startled, Captain jumped and turned toward Connor. His butt barely bumped into a large, decorative, Chinese vase that had been sitting on a display stand next to the end table. The vase was about 3 feet tall, and judging from the blue and white art-work, was most likely a Ming Dynasty replica or made to look like something from that time period. The vase began to wobble. It was obvious that the vase was getting ready to leave the display and go to the floor. Even if the vase was not expensive, an accident would have made Rachel aware that someone had been in her home. There were only seconds for decisions and actions. Connor knew he wasn't going to be fast enough with his bum leg. Daniel knew it too, and he dove across the smooth, hardwood floor. He slid the last few feet with his hands out. He had caught the vase right before it reached the floor. "Oh my gosh! Nice catch Daniel!" said Connor. "Sorry, Matey." said Captain, frowning as he slipped his magnifier back into his pocket. "It's okay, buddy. I'm just glad Daniel was able to catch it." said Connor. "Thank you, Daniel." said Captain. "You're welcome, Captain. Connor, before we put this big thing back, will you look down into it? I thought I heard and felt something rattle inside of it when I caught it." said Daniel. Connor walked over and looked down into the tall vase. "I do see something, but I can't reach down into that thing." said Connor. They meticulously laid it on its side, and then carefully lifted the bottom until the item slid out of the vase. It clattered onto the hardwood floor. Daniel and Connor looked at each other as if they were both two different alien species looking upon each other's strangeness for the very first time. Their eyes were wide as the saucers that they would have traveled in. Lying on the floor was an old-style flip phone of the exact same type and brand that the perpetrator that had shot Connor had been carrying.

Connor quickly grabbed the phone and pressed the power

button. The battery was low, but it came on. He pulled out his cellphone and looked up Daniel's burner phone number. "Look, Daniel, if there's any chance that this burner phone could be the one that we think it could be or if there's a chance that it's dirty, I don't want it connected to me in any way. I'm going to text your burner phone from this one, and you'll have the number. As soon as you can, forward the number to me, and then you need to find out the burner phone number of our perp from the motel and the other number he had been communicating with. I'll delete the history from this burner as soon as I text you from it, so Rachel would not see that it had sent a text, just in case she checks it for some reason." said Connor with a sense of urgency. Daniel nodded. Connor texted Daniel's burner phone from the one from the vase and then deleted the history after he had done so. He powered the phone back down and replaced it inside of the vase. After putting his own cellphone away, he and Daniel righted the vase and replaced it on the display stand. "We've got to go." said Daniel. They gave the apartment a cursory glance, hoping that they had been careful during their search, and then left, with Daniel locking the door back as it had been. As far as they could tell, they had been unnoticed during their entry and exit from the apartment. They all jumped into Daniel's sedan, and Daniel left as quickly as he dared in order to not draw any unnecessary attention. "Guys, if I take you back to your office, I may not make back it in time." said Daniel. "Go straight to the motel, we'll get a ride back to the office, don't worry." said Connor. Daniel nodded and ventured to speed up a little. Even though he was a cop, he didn't want to draw any attention to them.

Right before they got to the motel, Daniel stopped and let the Gellar men out of the car. "Sorry, guys." said Daniel. "It's okay, get going. Make sure you text me that number *tonight!*" exclaimed Connor as he slammed the door shut. "I will." said Daniel and then sped away. Connor pulled out his cellphone and called a taxi. He and Captain went back to the office.

When Daniel got to the motel, he rapidly pulled into his previous parking space, hopped out of the car, and sprinted toward the room where Rachel was. After he got to the room, he quietly unlocked the door and slipped inside. With relief, he could see the gentle rise and fall of the cover that was draped over Rachel as she was breathing. As he did before, he quickly, but quietly, undressed and then as motionless and scrupulously as possible, replaced her house keys from where he had retrieved them, and then carefully slipped into the bed on the side opposite the way that Rachel was facing. Other than her breathing, she did not move a muscle. Daniel was extremely proud of himself not only for today's accomplishments, but for pulling off his sham with Rachel not once, but twice. Rachel, who still faced away from Daniel, opened her eyes. Although she had slept through Daniel's exit from the room, she had been completely aware of his sneaky reentry. Her face was very thoughtful and carried a look of petulance. She closed her eyes once again and continued to feign sleep.

| 19 |

Chapter 19: Daniel's Dilemma

It was the end of their shift, and Daniel was driving Rachel home. He didn't have to pretend to be in good spirits. His positive frame of mind was from the progress that he, Connor, and Captain had made today. If Captain wouldn't have bumped into that vase, they would not have obtained the possible lead they had. If their suspicions of the connection between the burner phones were correct, it could still possibly be the end of his marriage and his career, but at least this mess would be all over. However, if they were able to prove that he had been set up and railroaded, there could still be forgiveness from his wife and maybe even the department. Rachel was not much of a talker, and the ride to her apartment building had been a quiet one. Daniel pulled into the parking space that he and the Gellar men had been in only a few hours earlier. "Alright, partner, I'll pick you up in the morning at the usual time." Daniel said. Rachel's demeanor had changed from that of a quiet, demure librarian to that of an alluring, jungle cat in a matter of seconds. She turned toward Daniel and jumped into his lap, facing him. She then kissed him roughly, while holding her hands on each side of his head. "I'm still hungry, Daniel. Let's go to the park." she whispered, sensually, as she slid back into the passenger seat. He knew this had not been a request. Daniel had come to know her well enough to know that she would not be taking "no" for an answer. She would not accept any excuses from him. Any attempts to reason with her for his need to attend to other demands in his life fell on apathetic ears. "I'm going to freshen up. I'll be right back." she said, as she got out of Daniel's car. Daniel pulled out his personal cellphone and called his wife. "Hi, honey." he said. There was a brief pause. "Look, I'm sorry, but I'm going to be home late again to-night." he continued, dejectedly. Daniel's eyebrows furrowed with heartache as he listened to his wife's despondent and disappointing response to the additional lies he kept piling upon her.

Rachel went into her apartment, went to her bedroom, and quickly picked out a fresh set of clothes. In fact, she chose a brand-new outfit, that was provocative, not like the pant-suit she currently wore. She picked up the outfit's matching clutch and then headed to the bathroom. She stripped her clothes off and speedily dressed in her fresh outfit. Because the three men had been so careful, she did not notice any-thing out of place. Unfortunately, they had not had time to search her apartment as thoroughly as they had hoped due to the time constraints they felt had been pressing down on them. This fact became evident when Rachel pulled up the register on the bathroom floor. She reached inside the opening, extended her arm down the air duct, and retrieved a small revolver. She replaced the register, stood up, and placed the gun in the clutch she was carrying. She picked up a bottle of perfume, sprayed herself a few times, and then headed out. As she approached Daniel's car, through the open window, she heard him on the phone with his wife. "Well, honey, I really have to go now." he said. There was a brief pause. "Okay, I'll see you sometime tonight." he continued. After another brief pause, he said "I love you. 'Bye." and then hung up. She waited until he had disconnected the call before she got into his car. She could see the anxiety on Daniel's face. "She'll get over it." said Rachel, unemotionally. As far as she was concerned, the only true love there had ever been was the love her parents had shared until they were ripped away from her. Daniel looked over at Rachel. Even though he was just as much to blame for their affair as she was, he so much wanted to ask her how she could be so heartless. When he saw the outfit she had on, he guiltily knew the reason why he didn't. Daniel headed for *Fresh Breeze Park,* only a short drive from her apartment building.

After the taxi had dropped Connor and Captain off at the office, the two Gellar men headed home. The day had been very stressful. He felt as if they needed to relax and unwind. It was a little earlier than their usual time, but they picked up some take-out food, went home, and had supper while they watched a movie. He tried his best to concentrate on the movie, but he couldn't get the day's events off of his mind. He kept checking his phone. He knew that Daniel had said it was difficult to get a moment's privacy to use the burner phone, but with something as important as this, Connor figured he would have tried harder to get that number to him as soon as possible. It still would be of little use until Daniel retrieved the numbers from the burner phone at the department, but Connor had always been the type that loved to have another thing checked off of his list. He and Captain went to bed early. Even though Connor was very tired, he could not sleep. After Captain had begun to slumber, he carried his cellphone with him to his home office and fired up the computer. He pulled up the photos he had taken of the front and back of the picture in Rachel's apartment. He zoomed in on the back of the picture so he could see the characters better. There were many resources on the internet available that displayed Chinese characters, along with their meanings. After a little while, he had finally found everything he was looking for. He found the symbol for *father*, which, according to the internet resources, was pronounced: "foocheen." He also found the symbol for *mother* and it was pronounced: "moocheen." It turns out that was not just Rachel's mother's nickname, but her designation as well. Out of curiosity, Connor looked up the Chinese word for *daughter.* He found the symbol for it as well. Sure enough, it was, indeed, pronounced "new-arr," the same as the nickname that the old man had said Rachel's mother had called her.

Daniel knew the well-concealed spot at *Fresh Breeze Park* all too well. He had visited it many times as a teenager and then had chased off many teenagers once he had become a cop. With it being so close to Rachel's apartment building, it was a place she liked to go, as it was very convenient. She liked the excitement of being in public, even though Daniel would say *What will someone do if they see us, call the police?* The park had not yet closed when they had arrived, but Daniel knew the trick on how to get by the gate should they get locked in. As it was vacant, he slowly pulled his sedan into the concealed area. Even though it was still not yet dusk, Daniel still turned off the headlights. He switched the motor off and looked over at Rachel. From how she had acted earlier, he expected her to immediately initiate relations. She didn't even look at him and was oddly quiet. After an awkward silence, even for her typical quirkiness, Daniel finally spoke. "Rachel, what's wrong?" She still didn't look at him and continued her silence. "Rachel?" he asked. "Where did you go today?" she asked, still not looking at him. Daniel's heart sank. "What are you talking about?" he asked. She turned to him and screamed, "Don't treat me like I'm stupid, Daniel!" He flinched with startlement. He knew all too well that stupid was something Rachel definitely was not. His mind scrambled to come up with an explanation. He knew he should have already come up with some kind of cover story for leaving beforehand, but they had been so hard-pressed for time. His hesitation and silence were all that she needed. "I thought that we had something, Daniel. I thought that you liked me." said Rachel, switching gears from being loud and hotheaded to soft-spoken and composed. "I do . . . I do like you, Rachel. But what you've been doing . . . what *we've* been doing is not right." said Daniel. "You're like everyone else. You use people and get what you want or need from them. When you've had enough, you toss them aside like trash." she said. Daniel wanted to tell her the same thing. He wasn't going to deny that he had enjoyed their intimate times together, but he wanted to tell her that he felt as if *he* was the one that had been used. He wanted to tell her that it was *her* that had started this all. When he saw that she had a gun in her lap, and pointed at him, he decided he would not tell her those things. In fact, he was thinking harder than he ever had in his life about what he *was* going to say.

Connor printed out the pictures from his cellphone of the front and back of the photo of Rachel's parents, along with the few pages of research he had done on the Chinese characters. He powered down his home office computer, picked up his cellphone and printouts, went by the kitchen, and got a bottled water. He took a few swallows and then headed to the bedroom. Captain was softly snoring. He sat his bottled water and the printouts on the nightstand. He checked his cellphone one more time. It was very late, and Daniel still had not texted him. That was the last thing they had discussed when Daniel had left them. Connor had told him to text the number to him tonight and Daniel had said he would. He knew that Daniel had told him that Rachel would sometimes want him to stay with her after a regular shift's end, and it was possible, that may have happened tonight. It was also possible that something was wrong. There was really nothing Connor could do but wait, otherwise risk possibly making the situation worse. He placed his phone on its nightstand charger and tried to get some sleep. He could not remember feeling this mentally exhausted since Alexis had passed away.

"Rachel? You're going to shoot me for leaving the room today?" Daniel asked. "Who knows about us, Daniel? Have you been talking to the SBI? Captain Lester? Your old partner, Connor?" Rachel asked, with paranoia. Daniel hoped that with the fading light, she had not seen him blink with the mention of Connor's name. "Let's talk about this, Rachel." Daniel said, calmly. "All you had to do is listen to me and enjoy yourself. But evidently, nothing is good enough for you." she said. Daniel could feel her anxiety building. "Rachel . . ." said Daniel reaching toward her. She raised the gun and he pulled his hands back. "Don't move, Daniel. I don't think I can trust you any more. I never could really trust *anyone.*" she said, hoarsely. Daniel could see that her eyes were becoming wet with tears. A single tear had finally managed to get out and slid down her cheek. "I never could really trust anyone." she repeated as she started to cry. Rachel's manner seemed to change from that of the tough, confident woman he knew to a small, frightened child, right in front of his eyes.

Daniel once again reached over to her in an effort to comfort her. She reacted by raising the gun and pointing it at him. He quickly cupped her gun-wielding hand in his, making no attempt to take the gun. "I just want to help you, Rachel." said Daniel. Their eyes locked and she looked into his deeply, for several moments, as if searching his mind and soul. Briefly, Daniel thought that she might accept his offer of help. Suddenly, she tried to pull her gun and hand away, from

Daniel's clasped hands. Daniel was still holding on to them when the gun went off. Daniel grunted, his eyes widened, and he relaxed his grip on Rachel's hand as he slumped over. "Daniel!" Rachel screamed. She dropped the gun and pulled Daniel back up to a sitting position. "Daniel, I'm sorry!" she exclaimed. There was blood spreading down his face from the top of his head. Rachel shook him, gently. "Daniel!" she shouted again. As she had been trained, she started to check his pulse when she saw a pair of headlights approaching in the distance, from the opposite side of the park. She was legitimately sorry. Even though there had been the possibility that she would have shot him, dependent upon the outcome of their discussion, this had been an accident. However, her unstable mental state and drive for self-preservation over-rode her sense, compassion, and ability to do the right thing. Panicking, but thinking quickly, she took his wallet and his service pistol, which was everything of any value in his car. She made sure she had her revolver and her clutch. Being Daniel's partner, she did not have to worry about her DNA being all over the place, as that would be normal. She got out of the car and began jogging back in the direction of her apartment building, making sure she was not seen.

Rachel made it back to her apartment uneventfully. Once inside, as a precaution, she not only placed her revolver in the bathroom air duct, she placed the clutch she had been carrying, Daniel's wallet, his service pistol, her shoes, and all of the clothing she had worn in there as well. Fortunately, the outfit had been comprised of a thin shirt and leggings. She made sure the items did not block the airflow. She knew she would eventually be getting rid of these things at her first opportunity. Being a police detective, she knew exactly what she needed to do to make sure she had not only cleaned and removed all of the gunshot residue from her hands but how to make it look as though she had not done so. *If everything goes down as it should, I would have done all of this covering up for nothing, anyway. But better to be safe than sorry.* she thought. Rachel finished her thorough preparations and cleaning, took a shower, and then went to bed.

Chapter 20: A Cop When You Need One

The headlights had belonged to Edmonton's finest. Maybe it was serendipity that a black and white had been dispatched to check the area due to reports of a vehicle spotted in the park after closing hours. These boys in blue were also aware of the park's nooks and crannies, and checked the spot where Daniel had parked. When the investigating officers found Daniel, they quickly called an ambulance. After calling in the license plate number, they soon found out that Daniel was one of their own, and called in the 10-999. The CSI team was dispatched. Daniel was still alive but was unresponsive. The ambulance took him to Edmonton General. The CSI team was unable to find anything useful outside, and they had Daniel's car towed to the police impound yard.

The following morning, about 30 minutes after Daniel's usual time to pick Rachel up from her apartment, which was very early, she placed a call to Daniel's phone. Unsurprisingly, it went straight to voicemail. Rachel spoke into her cellphone and said "Good morning, Daniel. I hope all is well, but I just wanted to check in with you. It's not like you not to be here promptly. I'll wait another half an hour for you to come or call, and then I guess I'll head to the department. 'Bye." and then she hung up the phone.

Connor heard some rustling and slowly opened his eyes. He turned toward the source of the sound and saw Captain standing next to him, using his magnifying glass to zoom in and out on the papers he had printed and laid on the nightstand before he went to sleep. "Good morning, Captain. Whatcha doin'?" asked Connor, sitting up in bed. "'Mornin' Matey, I'm 'vestigatin'." he said. Connor's brain was still a little foggy and it took him a few moments to process the fact that Captain had wakened before he did. That rarely happened. Unless Captain knew that Connor had to hurry in the morning, there was usually a morning routine of hugs, kisses, and a little coaxing before Captain rose. Sometimes, there was the *little mouse* routine where Captain would pull the covers over his head and make a squeaking sound. Connor would say *I hear a little mouse. Where's my little mouse?* When Connor's mind finally switched into high gear, he glanced at the bedside clock. He had overslept. He couldn't remember if he had any morning appointments or not. Was someone waiting for him at his office? *Had Daniel ever texted?* He reached over and grabbed his cellphone from the charger on the nightstand. He went straight into the calendar application. Connor was relieved that there were no appointments scheduled for today.

The flexibility of your schedule was definitely one of the main benefits of having your own business. *You could end up losing everything you own if you're not careful, but you can be late to work just about any time you want.* Connor thought, sarcastically. He looked through his text messages and found several inquiring about his services, but none of them were from Daniel. He looked at his missed calls. Most of them were numbers he did not recognize and they correlated with voicemails that were left. However, there was one that made his heart drop. It was Captain Lester's number.

Rachel glanced at her cellphone to see if it was time for her to head to the department. As she was looking at it, Captain Lester's number showed up on her screen as he was calling. She quickly answered the phone. "Hello? I was just getting ready to head to the department, Sir." said Rachel. "Rachel, Daniel was shot last night." said Captain Lester. "Oh, my! How is he doing? What happened?" she asked as if surprised. "They had to do emergency surgery last night. He's in the ICU at Edmonton General now." said Captain Lester. "I'm going to head there, now!" Rachel exclaimed. "Okay, I'm here now with Mrs. Bryson. I'll see you soon." said Captain Lester. "Okay, 'bye." she said.

Connor quickly pressed the button to return Captain Lester's call. He answered immediately. "Connor, I know you and Daniel seemed to be on the outs when you left us, but I thought you might want to know that he was shot last night." said Captain Lester. "Oh, no! Is he okay?" asked Connor. "He had emergency surgery last night and he's in the ICU now." said Captain Lester. "Which hospital?" Connor asked.

"Edmonton General." responded Captain Lester. "We'll be there as soon as possible. Thanks, Captain Lester." said Connor as he hung up. Connor looked at his son. "What is it?" Captain asked, seeing the concern on his dad's face. Connor did not want to upset his son, but he wasn't going to lie to him either. "Listen, Son, Daniel has been shot. He's in the hospital right now. We need to hurry, get ready and go see him." said Connor. Captain's demeanor changed to a more somber one, and he nodded. The two Gellar men expedited their morning routine and then headed to Edmonton General Hospital.

Captain and Connor followed the directions given to them by the hospital's information desk attendant. Connor wondered what Captain was thinking about. The last time they had been to this hospital was when Alexis had begun to get sick. They stepped off of the elevator and followed the signs to the ICU waiting area. They walked in and stopped, looking around the medium-sized waiting area. They saw a few strangers sitting in various chairs, and in one corner of the room, he saw Captain Lester standing near the ceiling-mounted TV watching the news, Mrs. Bryson and Rachel, were both seated nearby. They walked over to where the women were seated. Connor hugged Mrs. Bryson and Captain followed suit. "Hello, Mrs. Sandy." said Captain softly, as he often used a title with some people's first names. "Hello, Captain. It's good to see you." said Mrs. Bryson. "Good to see you." Captain said. Connor glanced over at Rachel with the intent to greet her. Their eyes locked briefly and a slight shiver went down Connor's spine. "Hey, Rachel." he said. "Hi, Connor." she said.

As it was no secret to anyone that knew him, Connor had loved being a police detective and he now loved being a private investigator. He didn't think of himself as anything above the ordinary, but he did feel as if he had always been pretty good at his job. He really did not know anything of Rachel's skills as a detective, but there had been nothing but good reports about her as an officer. Although he could be wrong, or if it was possibly the intuition that does make you good at detective work, that brief glance into Rachel's eyes had seemed to foster a silent communication between them. His eyes had told her *he knew that she was involved.* Her eyes had told him *she knew that he knew.*

Captain usually warmed up to everyone. Sometimes, strangers would initiate a new fellowship with Captain, and at other times, he would be the one to reach out to them, especially if he saw that he could do them some good, or at the very least, make them happy if they seemed to be down. Connor had often thought that some outside observers might believe that some of the people that Captain met were, in a sense, doing some kind of civic duty by engaging with someone with special needs. But Connor knew better. There was something so very special about his son, that almost everyone that had been touched by him or involved in his life in some way, had left with something in their hearts that made their lives better and richer.

Captain was also a ladies' man. Women and girls, typical and special needs alike, seemed to be drawn to him and his special charisma. He's always had a girlfriend since he was a child. A few of his sweetheart relationships had lasted for several years. Connor felt guilty because he had not been able to allot any quality time for Captain's current beloved since the passing of Alexis and the struggle to keep his business afloat. Connor left Captain standing in front of the two seated women as he walked over next to Captain Lester. Before addressing Captain Lester, Connor momentarily watched his son. Rachel had not offered to speak to Captain. Connor could see an internal struggle on Captain's face. Captain did not know this pretty woman or exactly how she fit into Daniel's life, but he knew that his daddy knew her, and he also knew that she was somehow a part of this situation. After the knowing looks Connor and Rachel had given each other, he wasn't about to introduce his son to her, polite or not. He was not entirely sure if they had ever met when he had taken Captain to the department in the past. He watched his son for a few more moments as he could see that Captain was contemplating whether to reach out to Rachel or not. Captain had finally decided there was nothing to be said at the moment and walked over to his dad and Captain Lester.

Connor shook hands with Captain Lester. "Captain, do you remember my other captain? Captain Lester?" asked Daniel. "Hey, Captain." said Captain Lester as he extended his hand for Captain to shake. "Hey, Captain Lester. We got the same name!" exclaimed Captain. Captain did shake his hand but turned it into a hug. Connor laughed internally as he watched his rugged, old police Captain blush slightly. "So, Captain Lester, have they given any news on Daniel's condition?" asked Connor. Captain Lester motioned for the men to take a few more steps away from the women, and then he began speaking in a low voice. "Well, the good news is that the bullet did not enter his skull. From the angle that it had impacted, it bounced off. The bad news is that your head can't always withstand such a traumatic impact without some injury. Right now, he is in a coma. They have been doing scans and running tests to see the extent of the damage and how to proceed with treatment. He's stable now, but the doctor did not want to get Mrs. Bryson's hopes up, so he basically told her it was a 50/50 chance that he would make it." said Captain Lester. Connor nodded somberly. "Is there anything that you can tell me about what happened since I'm no longer on the force?" asked Connor. "I wish there was something *to* tell, Connor, I really do. I *can* tell you the same thing that was given to the press this morning. It appears to be a robbery. Detective Bryson received a gunshot wound to the head. We currently have no suspects. Other than that, you know as much about it as we do." said Captain Lester. *Well, possibly a little more.* Connor thought.

With Captain following him, Connor walked back over to where the women were sitting. They both were sitting quietly staring at the floor. Mrs. Bryson looked up at Connor and Captain as they approached. Rachel continued looking at the floor. Sandy Bryson was a beautiful woman. She was not quite as tall as her husband, full-figured, with shoulder-length, red hair. Connor seemed to recall that Daniel had mentioned that she was more than 5 years younger than he, and she appeared even younger than that. Other than her eyes being red and swollen from crying, she was dressed to the T and could have easily been on her way to a fancy party somewhere. *With such a beautiful wife, how did he ever get into this mess?* Connor asked himself. The question was instinctive human nature, as Connor had actually seen all the scenarios from his work with the department *and* as a PI. He knew Daniel's story for how it had happened, but he had long since learned that looks often did not have a whole lot to do with infidelity.

Although a tougher task than it had been before the shooting, Connor knelt down to be at eye level with Mrs. Bryson, holding in the grunt of discomfort from his bum leg. Captain stood next to him and placed his hand on his dad's shoulder. "Sandy, I'm very sorry this has happened." said Connor as he took one of her hands. "I know I'm not on the force anymore, but we will do everything we can to help find out who did this to him. Please let us know if there's anything we can do for you." said Connor, squeezing her hand. Sandy looked back and forth between Connor and Captain. "Thank you, Connor." she said. She looked down at her feet uncomfortably, but then looked back up and continued to speak. "I know this is long overdue, but I want y'all to know how very sorry I am about Alexis. I don't know exactly what happened between you and Daniel, but he had said that you two had a falling out. I've never seen him so stressed out from work before, so when he told me that our family was not to communicate with your family anymore, I didn't want him to become any more stressed out and upset than he already was. This was a while before Alexis had passed. When she did, even though it had been a long time since I had called, I still should have then. I'm sorry for that, I truly am." she finished through tears.

Connor squeezed her hand again and Captain, who had teared up as well from thinking about his mother, gave her a hug. Connor patted him on the back as he hugged Sandy. Connor used the arm on the chair to pull himself back up to a standing position, and Captain prided himself in assisting his father. "Sandy, *this* guy right here is my best friend." Connor said, hugging Captain's shoulders. "But regardless of any falling out, I want you to know, Daniel will *always* be my *next* best friend. Please let me know if you hear anything." said Connor to Mrs. Bryson. "I will, Connor. Daniel is blessed to have a friend like you." she said. Connor smiled. "I guess I should be going. All of you, please let me know whatever you can." said Connor, as he raised his hand in farewell and exited the waiting room.

"Captain Lester, I guess I should be getting on to the department." said Rachel only moments after the Gellars had departed. "Very good, Harris. Go ahead and get yesterday's report completed, and make sure it's by the numbers. Samuels is going on vacation next week. Talk to Martinez, you'll be paired up with him, at least until Samuels returns." said Captain Lester. "Yes, Sir. See you, Sir." said Rachel. "Ma'am." said Rachel, acknowledging Mrs. Bryson. "Thank you for sitting with me." said Mrs. Bryson. "Yes, Ma'am." said Rachel. She left the waiting area. After a few minutes, Mrs. Bryson began to speak. "Captain Lester?" she asked. He walked over to where Mrs. Bryson sat and sat down in the chair that Rachel had vacated. "Yes, Mrs. Bryson?" he asked, putting his hand on her shoulder. "I'm sure as his Captain, you already know that since the shooting incident that led to the end of Daniel and Connor's partnership, along with Daniel getting Rachel as his new partner, Daniel has seemed very preoccupied and stressed out." she said. "Yes, I know that the incident itself, and everything that had transpired since then has been very hard on him. I also felt as if something was not entirely right, and I'm very sorry I did not speak to them both. I was hoping that it was just adjustment issues and that it was simply going to take some time to work out." said Captain Lester. "Captain Lester, I am embarrassed to tell you this, but I have felt like something more has been going on. As a wife, sometimes you just know these things." said Mrs. Bryson. Captain Lester nodded to affirm that he understood her. "Also, I don't know quite how to tell you this other observation . . ." she began. "Just say what's on your mind, Mrs. Bryson." said Captain Lester. "I don't want to be disrespectful, Captain Lester, but Daniel's new partner, Rachel . . . she's very polite and seems very smart . . ." began Mrs. Brsyon. "She has proven to be an exemplary officer." said Captain Lester. "I'm sure she has, but as for her people skills, something just seems very off." finished Mrs. Bryson. Captain Lester, again, nodded his acknowledgment of Mrs. Bryson's observation. Although Captain Lester actually agreed with Mrs. Bryson, he certainly was not going to say anything negative or unfounded about one of his officers.

| **21** |

Chapter 21: Walking Tightropes

As Connor and Captain got into their car, Connor noticed Rachel coming out of the front entrance of the hospital. He assumed that she was going to be heading to the department, which was exactly where he had planned on going. He had to figure out how to get there before her. If she was definitely guilty, she may attempt to thwart his efforts to try to get the information he needed and get into the impound lot. He had to get hold of Daniel's burner phone *and* find out the number of the burner phone that was on the perp that had shot him along with the number the perp had been communicating with. He wanted to know if Rachel was involved in that shooting and if so, why?

Connor sped toward the department as fast as he dared. He pulled into a space at the front entrance, and he and Captain hurried in. A few heads turned and looked at the pair. The people he did not know, turned back away and continued on with the work they had been performing. A few of them that recognized him offered a wave of greeting. One of them was Officer Pete Johnson. Officer Johnson had been working for the department as a dispatcher for quite a few years until he eventually went on to become a cop. It worked out well for the force because whenever their current dispatcher was out sick or needed time off, Officer Johnson was always willing to fill in. "Hi, Connor, Hi, Captain!" exclaimed Officer Johnson. He could see in Connor's eyes that he needed to speak to someone. "Y'all want to come on back with me to the dispatch room, and let that young man see where all the trouble usually starts?" he asked. "Absolutely." said Connor. Captain smiled. The two men followed Officer Johnson.

When they walked into the room, there was a young lady that Connor knew by the name of Eileen Benton standing in front of 6 active computer monitors. The monitors displayed various information, such as maps, a communications screen, a reporting screen, etc. They curved around with the curved desk so that the person in the center could easily view all of them. There was a chair in the central location of the curved desk, but she was standing, evidently briefly filling in for Officer Johnson while he was away from his station. She was wearing a headset and reading one of the monitors. "Unit 4, we have a possible 647 in front of *One More Time* consignment shop in front of 330 Main Street." said Eileen into the headset's microphone. "Copy that, Eileen. We had other vagrancy calls in that area just last week. I'm 2 minutes out." said the voice behind Unit 4. Eileen had the external speaker turned on so that Officer Johnson would be able to hear the dispatch that was just made so he would be aware of the details of the call. "Ten-four, guys, be careful." she said. "Roger that." said the voice. Eileen looked over at Officer Johnson, Connor, and Captain as she removed the headset and handed it to Officer Johnson. "Thank you, Eileen." said Officer Johnson. "Anytime, Pete." she responded. "Hi, Connor. Captain? Is that you? You've got a mustache and a beard now!" exclaimed Eileen. "Yyyyyyyep." said Captain, drawing the word out as he sometimes did. "Hi, Eileen." said Connor, smiling. "I heard about Daniel. He's tough as nails. He's gonna be fine." she said, putting her hand on Connor's shoulder. "I think so, too, Eileen, thank you for saying." said Connor. "Well, boys, y'all take care, I better get back to work." said Eileen. Officer Johnson placed the headset on his head. "I'd ask y'all to have a seat, but this is the only one in here." said Officer Johnson. "That's okay, Pete, we won't be here long." said Connor.

"So, Connor, you've got even more worry written on your face than when you went and got yourself shot. What's on your mind?" Asked Officer Johnson. Connor hesitated before he spoke. Although he had been friends with Pete for many years, and he considered him a good friend, he wasn't really sure of how far the boundaries of that friendship extended. He did not want to get Pete in any kind of trouble any more than he wanted to get himself in any. "Well, Pete, speaking of that shooting, in particular, you know, I read the entire case file on that robbery, and I also read Daniel's full report. As you know, I had to write a report of my own, as well." Connor began. Pete crossed his arms, and Connor could sense his curiosity. He cleared his throat and continued. "So, I already know all the information in the file and on the reports. I just can't remember a few pieces of that information that I really need to know." said Connor. "*Realistically*, you could have retained all of that information. But *technically*, since you are no longer a police officer, I could get in big trouble for telling you anything from that case or out of those reports." said Officer Johnson. "*Hypothetically*, no one would ever know that you did, because I just *might* have been able to retain all of that information. Who knows? Maybe I had made copies of the case files and reports while I worked for the department and kept them at home for study and review." said Connor, continuing the play on words. "*Theoretically*, if someone found out I had told you anything, I could get fired." said Officer Johnson with a final, but sobering play on words.

Connor nodded slowly with understanding, and exhaled with frustration. "Well, thanks, anyway, buddy. I apologize, I shouldn't have even had asked a friend for something like this. I'll let you get back to work." said Connor, disheartened. He found that he wasn't sure if he was more upset about not getting the information he needed, or from potentially jeopardizing a friendship. "Well, Captain, tell Pete 'bye, I guess we need to be heading out." Connor said. "Bye, Pete." said Captain, giving him a hug. "See ya, man." said Connor as he turned to leave. "You two, just hold up. I was kind of curious about some of the details in that file myself." said Officer Johnson. Both of the Gellars halted their retreat, then turned and faced Officer Johnson. He pulled the computer keyboard toward him and began typing. After a little typing and a few mouse clicks, all of the case file data popped up on one of the many computer screens. "Guys, please excuse me, nature calls again. If a call comes in, would you mind calling for Eileen down the hall?" said Officer Johnson, as he stood up and walked out of the room, not waiting for a response. This caught Connor off-guard, but after only a moment's hesitation, he jumped on the keyboard and quickly browsed all of the data available to him on the computer screen.

After only a few minutes, he had found what he needed. He found the phone number of the perp's burner phone and the number that phone had been in contact with. He quickly punched them in as notes on his own cellphone. As he was familiar with the system, he took the liberty of closing the computer files for Officer Johnson. After only a few more minutes, Officer Johnson returned to the dispatch room. He glanced at the particular monitor that had displayed the case files a few minutes earlier and saw it to be blank except for the computer's GUI operating system. "Well, boys, I hope you had a good visit, but I really need to get back to work." said Officer Johnson. "Thank you for the tour, Pete." said Connor, extending his hand. Officer Johnson took it and they shook. Officer Johnson nodded in acknowledgment and their eyes locked for a moment. Connor read in his face. *You are welcome, but please don't ask me to do something like this again.* The Gellar men left the room, then headed down the hallway toward the front of the department. Connor made sure to scan for signs of Rachel as they were leaving. *If she had been coming to the department, she should have been here already.* Connor thought. Connor and Captain both waved at the few employees that they knew as they headed for the exit. Once they were outside, in the parking area, he saw there was still no sign of Rachel. A terrible thought entered his mind. *Even if she didn't know about Daniel's burner phone, she was a very smart woman. The thought most likely crossed her mind that there could be something incriminating to her in Daniel's car. She may have headed straight to the impound lot.* Connor looked over at Captain and said "Hop in buddy, we need to get somewhere fast."

Connor had not driven as fast as he was now driving even when he had been in a black and white. He had to hear the blare of car horns as he ran a few stoplights. He was cornering his older-model sedan as if it was a race car. He weaved in and out of traffic, with a few maneuvers where he had even scared himself. Captain's eyes were wide and his knuckles had turned white as he held on to the center console with his left hand on the car's built-in handhold with his right. Connor kept his eyes on the road, but out of his peripheral vision, he had seen Captain glance at him a few times. He wanted to make sure his son did not panic, so he said "It's okay, partner, we can run like this because we're private investigators!" He saw Captain turn to face him. "Yeah, we get the bad guys!" Captain exclaimed, happily. Connor smiled a huge smile for his son to see, in spite of all the negative thoughts that were streaming through his head.

Fortunately, the police impound lot wasn't that far away, but Connor feared that every moment that went by was another moment Rachel was using to her advantage. He only slowed his vehicle back down to the posted speed limit as he approached the turn for the asphalt drive that led into the impound lot. As he turned in, he pulled down the drive that led to a keypad and intercom system atop a steel post, similar to the one at Duffield's estate. Instead of a beautifully ornamented wrought-iron gate, the automated gate here was a rolling chain-link fence gate, with barbed wire stretched across the top. As Connor approached the keypad, he was startled when the gate began rolling open. For a brief moment, he naively thought the gate was opening for him. He then saw that a vehicle that was exiting had triggered the pressure sensor causing the gate to roll open. The vehicle pulled through and the gate began to close back. The car began to pull up beside him, and the driver-side window lowered, indicating the driver's desire to talk. Connor lowered his window as the car pulled up beside him. If Connor's jaw would have dropped any further, he could have fit a cue ball in his mouth without it touching his teeth. Rachel was looking back at him.

"They say a shut mouth catches no flies. Yours seems to be wide open." said Rachel, almost cheerfully. Connor was stunned, but began regaining his senses, and slowly closed his mouth. "Fancy meeting me here?" she asked with somewhat of a blithe arrogance. "Yeah, something like that." Connor said, finally managing to speak. "Well, I had a feeling we would eventually bump into one another." said Rachel. They were both silent for a few moments. "Listen, Connor, it was an accident." Rachel added. "What was an accident?" asked Connor. He knew Rachel was talking about Daniel, and she was too smart to incriminate herself by the careless use of words. She ignored his question. "It's over now, Connor, just let it go." she continued. "Rachel, Daniel isn't dead. He has a good chance of making it. When he does, he's going to tell everything, no matter what it costs him!" snapped Connor. Rachel looked at Connor with sadness in her eyes. Connor's perception kicked in, and he had a feeling that she may already have a plan to make sure that he wasn't going to make it. "You had better stay away from Daniel." Connor threatened. Again, Rachel either ignored his comment or just chose not to acknowledge it. "The number was received but it never went back out. I now understand everything you guys were doing and what you have already done. CSI did an inventory list, they did a detailed search of the car, and they dusted for prints. However, I was a little more thorough than they were, as they had no real reason to dig into the places I did. It's over now, Connor, so just let it go . . . before you lose everything as Daniel will." Rachel said as she held up Daniel's burner phone. She only allowed Connor a brief glimpse before she lowered it once again. Before Connor could speak again, her window began to rise, and she quickly pulled away.

Connor's mind was racing as he turned the car around to pursue Rachel. They were in a real predicament. He wasn't an officer anymore; he was a private citizen. Where would he stand as a private citizen pursuing and possibly confronting a police officer? He currently had no evidence to even entertain the idea of a citizen's arrest. Rachel could probably get away with shooting both of them if he wasn't careful. Daniel's burner phone, which held the phone number of the burner phone from the vase at Rachel's apartment, and the phone in the vase itself was the only proof that Connor knew of that could tie her to the motel shooting incident. At this point, of course, the theory was just conjecture. Could she be heading to the hospital now? Or now that she is aware of their knowledge of her burner phone, could she be heading to her apartment to get rid of it? With Rachel's lead and all the side roads she had to choose from, Connor had to make a decision about where to go and what to do. They couldn't be in two places at one time. Surely, she had figured that Daniel was her loosest end that needed tying up, as he would be an eyewitness.

Rachel had already gotten too far ahead in order for Connor to follow her. As he maneuvered through the side roads of the neighborhood near the impound lot, he had made a decision on what to do. It was no longer a question of trying to keep Daniel or even himself out of trouble. Now, the most important thing was to save Daniel's life. He also wanted to make sure that Rachel did not get away with her crimes, and no one would ever be hurt by her again. With heavy apprehension, Connor pulled out his cellphone and called Captain Lester. Fortunately, he had the captain's personal cell number on his own personal phone, otherwise, he might have to wait, and maybe even been sent to Captain Lester's desk phone voicemail. Captain Lester answered Connor on the first ring. "Gellar? Is everything okay?" Captain Lester asked, as Connor very seldom called his personal phone.

"Captain Lester, Sir, I'm afraid nothing seems to be okay. I will explain everything later, but I'm really going to have to ask you to trust me with what I'm asking you to do." said Connor. "What is it, Connor?" asked Captain Lester, concerned. "Sir, I know this goes against every fiber in your being, and I could get into a lot of trouble if I was wrong, but

I have every reason to believe that Detective Harris not only shot Daniel, but could be, at this very moment, on her way to make sure he doesn't ever talk about it. Sir, I would really feel a lot better if we had some units posted at his room that will not let her near him." said Connor. "Connor, it sounds like you might be in trouble whether you are right about this or not. I'm not going to send any units . . ." began Captain Lester. "What? Captain, I'm serious about this!" exclaimed Connor, interrupting Captain Lester. "Calm down, and let me speak, Gellar. I'm not sending any units because I'm going to head back over there myself." said Captain Lester. Connor's anxiety levels dropped tremendously. "Thank you, Captain Lester, I'm sorry." Connor said, gratefully. "Whether you're right or wrong, Gellar, after dropping this in my lap, I have a feeling you won't be thanking me after we get this sorted out." said Captain Lester. "Yes, Sir." said Connor. "Where are you anyway, Gellar?" asked Captain Lester. Connor hesitated. Captain Lester, using more of his exceptional intuition, added "Look, Gellar, you know as well as I do, if you're right about her, and you're even thinking about trying to unlawfully obtain any potential evidence, you are running the risk of that very same evidence being inadmissible due to the exclusionary rule. Not to mention, ***you are no longer a police officer, you are a civilian, and you could be subject to criminal charges.***" Connor hesitated once again. "I understand, Sir." said Connor. There was a moment of silence, then Captain Lester said "Good luck, Connor." His ex-police captain's intuition never ceased to amaze him. Captain Lester may not have known the extent of what was going on with

Rachel and Daniel, but he knew *something* was going on. He had always tried to give his subordinates the benefit of the doubt and let them work out any of their own problems before resorting to departmental interference. "Thank you, Sir." said Connor, hanging up the phone. Since the captain was headed to the hospital, Connor and Captain were free to head to Rachel's apartment.

As he rolled into the apartment's parking lot, Connor scanned the area and saw no sign of Rachel's automobile. He again pulled into the space that they had used earlier. He switched off the engine. "Captain, get me the little black pouch from the glove box." he said. Captain opened the glove box and removed several items until he found the pouch Connor needed. "Captain, what we're doing now is against the law. But if we don't do it, other people like Daniel might get hurt, do you understand?" asked Connor. "Yes, Matey. I don't want nobody to get hurt." said Captain. "Okay, buddy, come with me and listen to everything I say, okay?" asked Connor to his son. "I listen." said Captain. They headed to Rachel's apartment. There were a few other residents going about their business, but no one seemed to be paying them any attention. Having been there before, Connor was already familiar with the old-style locking mechanisms on the door. Captain handed the pouch to his dad. Connor unzipped the pouch and found the lock picking tools he needed. In a matter of minutes, Connor and Captain were inside Rachel's apartment.

Not that it was a great plan, but it was all Connor could think of on such short notice. They were going to go into

Rachel's apartment, retrieve the phone from the vase, and hide it somewhere *inside* of the apartment. If things did go down that put Rachel in the crosshairs as a suspect, the phone would still be considered in her possession. They would have to be really on their game for hiding it well, as Rachel had already demonstrated her resourcefulness for finding things such as when she had found Daniel's burner phone. It was much darker in the apartment than Connor had remembered. All of the blinds were drawn and there were no lights switched on to provide any illumination. He found a light switch and flipped it, but the lights did not come on. Connor pulled out his cellphone and used its built-in flashlight. Although the light of the phone was bright, it had a limited reach. He could roughly remember the apartment's layout and the general location of the vase that held the burner phone. The apartment opened up into the living room, which was where the vase had sat. He made sure that Captain was on his heels, then he carefully headed in the direction of the vase. Captain followed him slowly and carefully. They maneuvered around some furniture and approached the area where Connor remembered the vase to be on display. He raised his cellphone, lighting up the end table. He panned the light over to where the vase stand was located. Connor's heart sank and then it began to beat rapidly. His face felt flush, and he could feel the hairs on the back of his neck stand up. The stand was there, but the vase was not. "Looking for this?" asked Rachel's voice from the dark. He turned with his cellphone-flashlight just in time to see the large vase in mid-swing by Rachel. He shoved Captain hard to push him away, as he tried to avoid the blow Rachel had been aiming at his head. From Connor's shove, Captain stumbled backward into the dark. Rachel was strong for her size, but the vase was heavy and bulky. She still managed a sufficient swing to knock Connor down. Unfortunately for Connor, his attempted avoidance made the impact of the vase even worse. Whereas the side of the vase was initially going to hit him, by managing to pull back slightly, the hard bottom of the vase caught him on the side of the head. The brief interruption of blood flow and the discharge of his brain's electrical impulses caused Connor to see stars as he went down hard to the floor.

Connor's head was hurting and throbbing. He had been surprised that the vase had not shattered from the impact against his head. *I'm surprised my skull didn't shatter, either.* he thought. His bum leg was also pounding from the fall he had taken. He was unsure if he had remained conscious for any length of time or had only blacked out momentarily from the bang against his head. He gently felt the side of his head, and there was a feeling of wetness on the tender area that had taken the brunt of the impact. *I'm bleeding.* he thought. Connor was disoriented, and the light shining on his face did not help any. He could barely make out Rachel's silhouette behind the glare of the flashlight she had pointing at him. She was holding the flashlight against her temple and had a handgun trained on him. "Captain? Are you okay?" Connor shouted out. "I okay, Matey. You hurt?" Captain's voice came out of the dark from the direction Connor had pushed him. "I'm fine, son." said Connor directing his voice toward Captain. He turned his head back toward Rachel. "Rachel, please don't hurt him." said Connor. "*I fine, Matey.*" Captain assured him, again, with persistence. "Don't you worry, Connor. I would never dream of hurting your sweet boy . . ." began Rachel. Connor had a slight sense of relief, but knew there was no possible way things were going to turn out good. "However, his dad just broke into my home, so I'm afraid he's not going to be so lucky." she finished. Although Connor could not see her clearly due to the flashlight aimed at his face, he could tell her body language had tensed. He felt as if she was, indeed, preparing to fire her weapon. All the while they had been conversing, Connor had been slowly moving his hand closer to the lapel on his jacket, and closer to the gun he carried in a shoulder holster under it. Rachel may be mentally unstable, but her skills had never faltered. "I wouldn't do that, Connor. Things may turn out even worse for you than they already seem to be. Keep your hands away from that gun and where I can see them. I had told you to just let it go, but you wouldn't listen." she said, calmly. He stopped his hand from moving toward his weapon, and slowly moved it back away. He had a slight feeling of déjà vu, as this scenario was so similar to the shooting incident in which Daniel had saved his life. Only this time, Daniel was laid up in the hospital.

Connor again had a feeling of foreboding. Although he knew that Rachel would realize he was stalling, he also did want to get some answers. He asked "Can you just tell me *why*, Rachel? Why this obsession with Daniel, and why did *I* have to get shot?" She didn't respond. "At least tell me why you had me shot!" exclaimed Connor. "Because that was the only way I was ever going to get to be with Daniel!" she exclaimed. No phone verification needed now. She was definitely behind the shooting, as they had suspected once they had seen that burner phone. "He would have never even looked at me as long as you were his partner! I knew he would want me if he just gave me a chance! And then, I made him pay dearly for that!" she shouted. He could hear Rachel's voice wavering. "But why? And why Daniel?" Connor asked, quietly, as much to himself as to Rachel. She was quiet once more. Connor quickly thought back through all of the investigation that he and Captain had done of Rachel when it suddenly dawned on him. He thought back to when they were in Mrs. Peterson's home and Captain had spotted that picture of Otis Peterson. It had resembled Daniel so much it was uncanny. He was no psychologist, but everything that had happened with Daniel and Rachel just didn't add up or make any sense. He felt that maybe Rachel was experiencing some sort of transference from her past with her abusive step-parent Otis, to the present with Daniel. She had been through so much trauma, her mind was finally finding a way to help her deal with it. "Is it because Daniel is so much like Otis Peterson?" he asked calmly. The once steady flashlight beam wavered with the mention of Otis' name. "Don't even mention that name!" she shouted. He saw her gun-hand arm extend toward him as if daring him to mention Otis again. "Okay, okay. I won't say his name again." said Connor.

"They are all alike. They are supposed to be people that you can trust. They are supposed to be the good guys. But in the end, they will just use you for what they want to, with no care about how it makes you feel or what it does to you." said

Rachel. Connor could hear quivering in her voice. "Rachel, I know some of what you went through as a child. But Daniel had nothing to do with that." said Connor. "He used me, too!" shouted Rachel, extending her arm once again. Connor could see her arm shaking in the flashlight beam. He held his arm up protectively in front of his face. When a gunshot did not come, Connor spoke again. "Rachel, I'm so sorry that those things have happened to you. It's still not too late to get some help." he said softly. He could now hear that Rachel was softly crying, but seemed to be attempting to keep it quiet. "I'm afraid it is. I've gone too far to turn back now. Daniel is probably going to die, but I truly didn't mean to shoot him. You think they would believe me? I'll just shoot an intruder and get rid of all of the evidence against me. I'll either get away with it or I won't. I don't care anymore." she said through stressful tears. "Rachel . . ." Connor began as she extended her arm once again. She began to squeeze the trigger.

Chapter 22: Speak of the Angels

Before she pulled the trigger, a brilliant light pierced the darkness behind Connor. While Connor and Rachel had been talking, Captain had made his way around the perimeter of the living room, in the dark, to the end table that held Rachel's decorative, Chinese figurines. Captain had picked up the same figurine that he had been examining when they had been in her apartment before. It was the Chinese woman wearing a kimono. He had held the figurine in front of his magnifying glass and had turned on his cellphone's flashlight. The light bounced off of the lacquered figurine, created a sparkling effect, and was magnified brightly behind Connor. The way the light shone through the magnifying glass with the sparkles scattered around, created a breathtaking, ethereal-looking depiction of an angel hovering in the air. Rachel was startled, but also amazed at the spectacular apparition. She hesitated and relaxed her trigger finger. Connor, still lying on the floor, craned his neck to see behind him. The hovering light reminded him of the dream of Alexis as an angel. "No shoot my daddy. He's my Matey. I love my daddy. Mommy is my angel now. Mommy loves me and daddy. Moochen is your mommy. Moochen is *your* angel now. Moochen loves you. Moochen no want you to hurt anybody." said Captain as he walked forward out of the shadows. He had lowered his magnifying glass, the figurine, and his cellphone light just enough so that he could see where he was going. He walked up to Connor, leaned down, gently touched Connor's head where he saw the blood, then kissed his dad on the forehead. He then walked over to Rachel who was still shakily holding the gun. Captain held up the figurine in front of Rachel. It sparkled in the beam of her flashlight. "This Moochen?" he asked Rachel as he offered the figurine to her. Rachel nodded. "Yes, that's Moochen." she said shakily, staring at the figurine with fresh tears sliding down her cheeks. "That's my Matey, and I his Captain. He no want *me* to hurt anybody, either." said Captain, motioning to his dad.

Rachel felt the strength leave her legs, and she knelt down on the floor. She laid her weapon and the flashlight to the side and took the offered figurine from Captain. She began sobbing. Although the flashlight was lying on the floor, it still provided enough light for Connor to see Captain standing beside Rachel. Connor squinted to see his face. Captain was watching Rachel intently as she knelt on the floor, crying. She held the figurine lovingly against her chest. Even though the area was dimly lit by the light of the flashlight, Connor could still see the wheels of his son's mind turning. Because he knew his son so well, he saw that Captain had finally made the decision that *now* was the right time to reach out to Rachel. He knelt on the floor in front of her, reached around her neck, and hugged her. She immediately put her arms around him and cried harder. "I'm so sorry, Captain, I'm so very sorry." she said. Captain rubbed her back and said "It be okay, Rachel."

Sirens in the distance announced the arrival of two marked units, along with Captain Lester's unmarked sedan. They pulled into the lot of Rachel's apartment complex. As Captain Lester and the four uniformed officers were getting out of their vehicles, Rachel's apartment door opened, and the three people that were inside came out the door. Connor, who was unable to walk by himself at the moment, was supported by Captain on one side, and Rachel on the other. Captain Lester and the officers met them in the parking area. "How did you know where we were?" Connor asked. "Daniel has come out of his coma. He told me everything. I had a hunch that you would be here, but I had gotten a search warrant anyway." said Captain Lester. Two of the uniformed officers took over assisting Connor. The other two began reading Rachel her rights and placing her in handcuffs. "Hey, take it easy with her, please. Captain Lester, I know she has done some terrible things, but there's more to the story than even Daniel knows yet. I want to see that she gets some help, and if I know Daniel like I think I do, he will want to see to that as well." said Connor. Captain Lester looked at Connor with raised eyebrows. To Connor, his look clearly stated *I believe you have run out of favors, so why are you even asking me for anything?* Even after giving Connor that look, Captain Lester said, gruffly "Treat her with respect, boys, and make sure nothing happens to her." With his head pounding and leg throbbing, Connor still managed a smile. "Thank you, Captain Lester." he said. "Look, in light of everything that's happened, after you go to the hospital and get treated, I'm going to let you go home, but don't leave town, Connor. You and Daniel have a lot more explaining to do, and I'm sure it's not going to be good." said Captain Lester. "Yes, Sir." said Connor, as he looked over at Rachel. One of the officers had his hand on the top of her head and was helping her into the backseat of the police cruiser. "We're going to get you some help, I promise!" exclaimed Connor. Rachel looked at Connor and briefly nodded in acknowledgment, but Connor could see in her eyes that she did not believe him.

The doctor reported that Connor had a slight concussion and had received stitches and a bandage for the cut on his head. His bum leg injury, although extremely painful, had only been superficial, and no further damage had been done. Alexis' friend, Francis, had been kind enough to come to the hospital long enough to sit with Captain until they were through running all of Connor's medical tests and had him patched up. "Who's with David, now?" asked Connor. "His friend Jerry is with him now. He said he didn't mind sitting with him while I ran up here with you two for a little bit. He knows David is a flight risk." said Francis, chuckling. "How is he doing?" asked Connor. "He's doing pretty good. He still can't be left alone, of course. I'd say about the same, as before,

I guess." she said. "I'm sorry I've not been able to help you after all the help you had given me." Connor said. "My goodness, Connor, we're an old, retired couple. About as much excitement as we have now is going to the grocery store. I think right now, we can manage. You boys still have busy lives to live." said Francis, smiling. Connor had been cleared to go home. He and Captain gave Francis hugs and thanked her for coming up. She left the hospital, and the Gellar men headed to the nurse's station to see if they could find out what room Daniel was in.

As they approached Daniel's room, Connor saw that there was a uniformed officer sitting outside of his room. He supposed Captain Lester had left him there for good measure. The officer recognized the Gellars and allowed them into the room. When they walked in, to Connor's surprise, Mrs. Bryson was asleep in one of the big recliners that some hospitals provide for a patient that is allowed an overnight guest. They quietly walked over to Daniel's bed. He was watching TV with the sound turned so low you could barely hear it. Daniel looked over at them. "Daniel!" Captain exclaimed in a whisper. "Hey, buddy." Daniel whispered back to him and took his outstretched hand. Daniel looked up at Connor, questioningly. Connor put his hand around both of theirs. "I'm glad you're okay, partner." whispered Connor. Daniel's eyes glistened. "I'm sorry, Connor. I should have never dragged you into this." whispered Daniel. Connor raised his eyebrows. "Nobody drags me into anything." whispered Connor. "Well, except for you, son." he added in a whisper. Captain looked at him, smiling. Connor turned and looked at the sleeping Mrs. Bryson and then back to Daniel, expectantly. "She's a jewel, Connor. She's stayed here with me the whole time. I had told her and Captain Lester everything, and I mean everything. I know I had said I was going to keep your name out of this, but that was until I got shot. I am very sorry, but I was scared you and Captain might get the same." whispered Daniel. "It's okay Daniel. I had already gotten my shot of lead first, though. She admitted she had set me up for that shooting, just to get the opportunity to partner up with you." whispered Connor. "So, that was the mate to the phone recovered from that perp?" asked Daniel, quietly. "Yes, it was. So, what did Sandy have to say to you after you told them everything?" asked Connor, keeping his voice low. "Sandy's the best, Connor. Of course, she was upset, and she told me that she already knew that *something* was going on. But she really loves me, man . . . and she told me . . ." whispered Daniel, hoarsely, as tears began to slide down his face, and he began to choke up from emotion. "I told him that under these circumstances, I do forgive him because I love him so much." began Sandy Bryson. She had woken up sometime during their conversation. Connor and Captain released Daniel's hand and turned to face her. "But I also told him that if it ever happened again, for *any* reason, it was over." Sandy stood up and walked toward the two men next to Daniel's bed. Connor and Captain both gave her a hug. She went to Daniel's side and kissed him on the cheek and squeezed his hand. "We're going to go and let you get some rest, Daniel. When you're on your feet again and up to it, we've got a lot to talk about and a lot we need to discuss with Captain Lester."

said Connor. Daniel nodded. They all said their farewells, and then Connor and Captain headed out of the hospital.

That night, after Connor and Captain had finished watching one of their TV shows and had prepared for sleep, before turning off the screen, Connor pressed the mute button, and turned to his son. "Captain, what you did today was very brave. You have done such a great job with me and I am so very proud of you. Do you understand that you saved your dad's life today?" asked Connor. Captain looked at Connor and nodded. "Daddy, you my Matey, and my partner. We take care of each other. I no want you to go up there." said Captain, as tears spilled down his cheeks. Connor hugged his son tightly. "I'm not going anywhere right now, my buddy." said Connor. Captain usually referred to heaven as "up there," and oftentimes when he thought of the potential passing of a family member that he cared for, it would bring back a flood of emotions for the other family members he had lost. After Captain's tears subsided, Connor released his son from his embrace. "Son, Daddy is going to be around a long, long time. Don't even think about it right now. Just always remember, no matter what, that Jesus is our Lord and Savior and He died for our sins. When it's our time to go up there, we'll go. And we will see each other again." said Connor. Captain rubbed his eyes as he nodded. The melatonin was starting to kick in. "I wanted you to know how happy I am that you are my partner and what a great investigator you are! We are going to have even more adventures together!" exclaimed Connor as he ruffled his son's hair. That brought back the smile that Connor longed to see. Although he was fighting sleep, Connor could already see his son's imagination going to work as he looked into his bright, blue eyes. Captain puckered his lips, indicating that he was ready for sleep and wanted his goodnight kiss. Connor kissed his son and it was only a few minutes later that Captain was softly snoring. Connor stroked Captain's hair and soon fell asleep himself.

| **23** |

Chapter 23: Truths and Consequences

Over the course of two weeks, Daniel had been released from the hospital and Connor had many phone conversations with him and Captain Lester. After Connor had explained Rachel's past to Daniel, they had both agreed not to press charges against her if she received counseling and therapy. Captain Lester, being the big softie that he was on the inside, called in some favors and did some pulling on the strings, and saved everyone's bacon to some extent, in one way or another, concerning each of their individual situations. Since Daniel did not press charges, and in light of Rachel's mental health, Captain Lester convinced the prosecutor not to press charges either. She was terminated from the force, but she did not go to jail. With her degree in criminal justice, there would be many opportunities for a career that was not police-related if that was the path she chose to take. Daniel was given an unpaid suspension for three months with a reprimand of misconduct placed in his file. Files of this type were rarely seen outside of the police department, so he was thankful for that. Connor was very fortunate. Based on the circumstances, he was not charged with anything and therefore got to keep his PI license. Connor was extremely grateful, as he had already lost so much.

Captain Lester had called Connor and asked him if he could come to the station, speak with him and sign a few papers. He and Captain went to the department after lunch and met Captain Lester in his office. When the two Gellars went into Captain Lester's office, he was typing away on his computer and never even looked up. Connor approached the desk and stopped with Captain on his heels. "Close the door, Gellar." said Captain Lester in his gruff, matter-of-fact voice. Captain Gellar heard the door close, but out of his peripheral vision did not see Connor move. He looked up from his computer, and saw Connor standing in front of him, with Captain by the door. "Oh, I was talking to your dad. Thank you, Captain." said Captain Lester with a gentler tone. "You welcome, captain." said Captain, grinning. "With all these captains in here, we're libel to get confused." said Captain Lester, feigning grumpiness. "You men have a seat." he added. There were more than enough guest chairs in Captain Lester's office, and the two Gellars sat in the ones closest to his desk. "Well, Connor, at your request, and from the discussions I've had with Rachel, I also believe that this Bentley Duffield did indeed abuse Rachel. I spoke to one of my friends at the FBI. She and I have helped each other out with various things over the years. I told her the story of Rachel's life and background, and about Bentley Duffield's contracts and involvement in federal projects, and she did some digging. With the abuse taking place on federal grounds, this would definitely be their jurisdiction. However, as much as we all want to get some justice and closure for Rachel, the fact of the matter is, that in federal eyes, he is a prominent member of society and has helped with many of those federal projects over the years." said Captain Lester. Connor stood up. "Yeah, while he was helping himself to an innocent girl!" exclaimed Connor, turning red. Captain Lester looked up at Connor with a stern look on his face but remained quiet. Connor sat back down. "Sorry, Sir, I.m just frustrated." Connor said. "I understand. Based upon Rachel's statements alone, there will be no investigation . . ." started Captain Lester. Connor started to get up again, but Captain Lester held up his arm vertically and made a fist, indicating that he wanted Connor to stop. Connor remained in his seat and Captain Lester continued. ". . . but if there were any solid evidence that could be provided or an admission of guilt, they *would* open an investigation." finished Captain Lester. "After eight years, I really don't think there's going to be any evidence. You remember how slick I told you Duffield was to avoid saying anything that would incriminate himself. How are we supposed to get an admission of guilt?" asked Connor. Captain Lester placed his elbows on his desk while interlocking his fingers and leaned forward. "You're the PI." he said, bluntly.

"And, meeeeeeee." said Captain, dragging the word out. "Of course, you too, Captain. You're the *best* PI and biggest hero we've had around here in some time." said Captain Lester, as he stood up. He walked around to where the Gellars sat in the guest chairs. He unfastened one of his captain's pins from his collar and fastened it to the collar of the knit shirt Captain was wearing. "Heroes need one of these. Now, not only is your nickname *Captain,* but you *are* a captain." said Captain Lester, clapping Captain on the back. Captain Lester went back around and sat back down behind his desk. Captain pulled his collar out where he could see the rank insignia. "Matey, look! Captain!" he said, excitedly. "Wow, buddy, wasn't that nice of Captain Lester!" exclaimed Connor. "Thank you, Captain Lester!" exclaimed Captain. "You're very welcome." said Captain Lester. Connor and Captain Lester nodded at each other with a silent understanding of thankfulness. Captain Lester took a breath and let it out slowly.

Connor nodded slowly. "Sir, that, of course, would be wonderful, if we could get an admission. But Bentley Duffield lives in a technological mansion and is very cautious about who he talks to and what he says. Not to mention the guy is an . . ." started Connor. Captain stood up and walked around behind Captain Lester's desk, cupped his hand over one of Captain Lester's ears, and whispered something. When Captain pulled back, Captain Lester looked at him with raised eyebrows and said "He's one of those, huh?" Captain nodded and bluntly said "Yes." Captain walked back to his chair and sat down. "Yes, he's definitely one of those." Connor confirmed. "Well, I don't want to know any details. If you do get any evidence or an admission, here's her name and number. Believe me, she would love nothing more than to take this guy down, but her hands are tied without evidence or a confession. Good luck." said Captain Lester as he handed Connor the scrap of paper that he had written the name and number on. "Thank you, Sir." said Captain. Captain Lester and Connor both looked at him with surprise. "Dismissed." said Captain Lester, smiling.

On their way home, Connor called Daniel and filled him in on what Captain Lester had told the two Gellars and what they had discussed would be necessary to be able to open an investigation of Bentley Duffield. "So, what are you going to do? Do you have a plan yet?" asked Daniel. "I have one forming in my head. I hope to have most of the details worked out by the time we get to Torrenceville on Wednesday. We will be going to Duffield's place on Thursday." said Connor. Daniel was quiet for a few moments and then asked "What can I do to help?" Connor was even more surprised to hear those words from a man that had been shot by Rachel than he was surprised at himself for helping her after she had hired someone to shoot *him*. "Daniel, buddy, I am very thankful for you, but you've not been long out of the hospital and you've been temporarily suspended from the force. One more screw up, and you may be out of a job." said Connor. Daniel reluctantly agreed and wished Connor good luck.

| **24** |

Chapter 24: Black Ops and Big Flops

Connor and Captain headed to Torrenceville, the hometown of Bentley Duffield. "Go where?" Captain asked him. "We're going on a secret mission, buddy. But before we do, how about if we go see that nice server, Annie, at *The Torrenceville Taste*, and we have some lunch? Country style steak for you, and a *Chicknado* for me?" asked Connor. "And mashed potatoes?" Captain asked, licking his lips. "Of course, mashed potatoes, silly." said Connor. Captain grinned and said, "Let's do it, Matey!"

When Annie saw the two Gellars walk into the restaurant, her face lit up. She ran to them and hugged them both. "I was wondering if I was ever going to see you two again!" she exclaimed. Connor's heart beat rapidly in his chest. Although still guiltily so, he was excited to be one of the objects of this beautiful woman's attention. He could feel his face flush but did his best to chase away the commingled feelings of embarrassment and excitement. Annie remembered the booth they had sat in the first time they had been in the restaurant, and since it was empty, she sat them there. She took their orders and put them in with the cook. She then went back to the booth and asked Captain if she could sit beside him. He slid toward the window and she sat down. Connor nervously reached across the table and cupped one of Annie's hands into his own. "Annie, I'm very sorry I haven't been back in touch with you. Captain and I both have really been through the wringer, lately. We've got one more big thing to try to take care of, and then hopefully, we can slow down a bit." said Connor. "We got a secret mission!" exclaimed Captain. "Shhhh. Don't let anybody hear you, or it won't be secret anymore!" said Connor in a whisper, half-joking with his son. "A secret mission, huh?" Annie whispered. "Yeah, seriously. We need to stay in town for a couple of days." Connor said, quietly. "Does this have more to do with Rachel?" Annie asked, quietly. "Yes, but let's not talk about it here." said Connor, quietly.

"Where do y'all plan to stay?" asked Annie. "I saw a little motel just outside of town that should do fine for just a day or two." said Connor. Annie hesitated and Connor could see in her face that she seemed to be contemplating something that was possibly uncomfortable when she finally said "Y'all could stay at my house. It's small, but there's plenty enough room and you'd have your privacy . . ." Connor did not answer right away. Captain turned to her. "Yeah, we stay with you, Annie." Captain said. "Whoa, there, Captain. We couldn't impose on you, Annie. Also, we have another person coming in later this evening." said Connor. "Rachel?" Annie whispered very lowly. Connor nodded. "Look, I know we don't know each other, in fact, we don't even know each other's last names, but I know what kind of people y'all are. I insist that you all stay with me." said Annie very quietly. It was several moments before Connor responded. "Are you sure, Annie?" Connor asked. "I'm positive. It's settled, then. I will take off after lunch and we'll go to my house." said Annie. "Thank you, *again,* Annie." said Connor. "Y'all are most welcome." she said. "It's *Gellar,* by the way. Our last name is *Gellar.*" said Connor. "Mine is *Brooks.*" said Annie, smiling. She retrieved Captain and Connor's lunches and they ate while Annie went back to her restaurant duties.

Annie's house was small, just as she had said. It was an older house but had been renovated. The yard was well-manicured and tidy. They found the inside of the house was also well taken care of. It was only a two-bedroom, but Annie's couch had a pull-out bed. Connor said that he and Captain could sleep there, and Rachel could take the bedroom. The two Gellars carried in not only their suitcases but several cases of equipment. Connor texted the address to Rachel, and she confirmed it. "Sorry about all this mess." said Connor, referring to their pile of cases and bags. "Goodness, don't worry about that. And y'all just make yourself at home." said Annie. "Thank you, Annie. I know you didn't really know Rachel, but I wanted to let you know, that she's already a changed person. I think for a long time that she had been putting on an act. But now, she's receiving counseling, therapy, and she told me she was on medication that makes her less anxious and helps her deal with the reality of her past. She said she can see things so much more clearly, now." said Connor. "Since the second time you two came into the restaurant, and we talked, I have tried to make it a point to stop judging people." said Annie. Connor smiled.

Rachel pulled into Annie's driveway in a large, older model, beat-up sedan a few minutes after 8pm. When she knocked on the door, Annie and the Gellars were seated in the living room. Connor looked at Annie. "It may make her feel more comfortable if y'all answer the door." said Annie. Connor nodded. He and Captian stood up, walked to the door, and answered it. Rachel gave both men a hug as part of her greeting, and Connor invited her inside. "This is our host, Annie Brooks." said Connor. Rachel shook hands with Annie. "Hi, Rachel, I know you don't know me, and it's been a long time, but I work at *The Torrenceville Taste.*" said Annie. "I do remember your face. I always wanted to eat there, but Bentley would never let us." said Rachel. "Well, you are going to get your chance when this mission is all over!" exclaimed Annie. Rachel smiled. "I'd like that." She said. Connor offered to help Rachel with her bags, but she only had one that she had brought in with her. After Rachel had settled into Annie's guest bedroom, they all gathered in the living room. "Well, I can give you all privacy if you would like." said Annie. "Actually, unless you'd rather not be involved, you are more than welcome to join us." said Connor. "Are y'all planning on hurting anyone or breaking any laws?" Annie asked, laughing. Connor rolled his eyes upward, and moved them from side-to-side as if trying to look around inside of his own mind, while he thought about her question. "Not planning to, but I can't make any promises. Technically, if things go as planned, the only law that we could be considered as having violated would be the encroachment up Duffield's driveway." he finally replied. "Well, count me in." Annie said. Connor was pretty sure that would have been her response regardless of how he had answered.

Connor went over the plan with his three cohorts. "Rachel has to convince Duffield to talk to her. If he doesn't talk, then our operation will be over before it even began. Unfortunately, if it should come to that, there will be nothing else we can do. But from what I sense about Duffield, he seems like the kind of man that would like nothing more than to talk to you, even if it's just for the enjoyment he gets from putting put you down. Rachel will be carrying a wireless transmitter. Since he is so paranoid, Rachel will also carry another recording device as a decoy. Something that he can find fairly easily if he searches her. That could actually work in our favor if he does find the decoy because it may give him a feeling of false security and that may help loosen his lips. Captain and I will be monitoring and recording the feed of the transmitter from the trunk of her car. We've already modified the trunk with a false bottom, just in case he has the car searched. The back seat of the car is basically a door that we can access to go to and from our area with our equipment in the trunk." said Connor. "What if he does search me? Where will I be carrying the actual transmitter?" Rachel asked. "Even though Duffield may have employees that do everything for him, I have a feeling that he may want to keep any dealings with you private. Whether *he* searches you or someone else does, hopefully, he will find our decoy and be satisfied. I'm going to need you to fix that long hair of yours in such a way that we can hide the transmitter in it. I think that's the best chance we have of it not being discovered." said Connor. "I can help with that." said Annie. "Excellent." Connor said, nodding.

"I think I have a general idea, but what do you think I could say to get him to start talking?" asked Rachel. "I have some ideas, also, but I'm afraid they will be painful memories for you." said Connor. "The memories are there, regardless." said Rachel, flatly. Connor nodded. Captain, who was sitting on the couch next to Rachel, put his hand on her back. She reached out and took his other free hand. "It was rumored, as Annie has filled me in, and I had confirmed by my own research, that after you left Torrenceville, along with some other incidents, you ended up getting involved with drugs. I think we should use that. You come crawling back to your wealthy ex-step-father to try to get money for drugs. And, of course, we can probably count on the fact that he is attracted to you." said Connor. Rachel nodded as she looked at the floor. Annie walked over to her and put her hands on her shoulders. "Honey, you've got nothing to be ashamed of. We've *all* had things happen to us and we've *all* done things in our pasts that we aren't proud of, whether it was from our own choosing or not." said Annie. Rachel looked up at Annie with glistening eyes. Annie gave her a comforting hug of reassurance. After a few moments, Connor continued. "Look, Rachel. You're in some good programs now. From the talks we've had lately, your outlook on life is the best it has ever been since you lost your parents. We don't have to do this. You can let it go, and move on with your life." said Connor. Rachel looked around the room at the three people who were there to help and support her. None of them were getting paid to do this. None of them were expecting anything in return. She had even been responsible for the gunshot to Connor's leg and come close to shooting him herself. Yet, here they were. For her. She wanted to cry as she was having a *There's still hope for humanity* moment, but for now, she pushed back the tears and focused her mind on the task at hand. After a moment, with a defiant look in her eyes, she said "Not just for me, but anyone that he has hurt since me, and anyone that he might hurt in the future . . . let's do our best to take that creep down."

The following morning, Annie treated them all to breakfast. None of the group was very talkative. Although the plan pretty much relied on Duffield's ego and there seemed to be no real danger involved, Connor sensed that a veil of foreboding had settled around the group. He felt as if the others may have sensed it as well. Even Captain, who was usually chipper, regardless of the situation, was not very talkative. He didn't even eat half of his eggs, grits, and livermush. After breakfast, everyone began to get ready and prepare themselves for their roles in the plan. After Connor and Captain were ready, they carried the equipment out to the large, old car that Rachel was driving, loaded, and set up the equipment in their secret compartment. Annie assisted Rachel with her preparations. "Rachel, you are naturally beautiful, but we don't want to make you look completely immaculate, otherwise, he may not believe that you're a desperate addict looking for a way to get your fix." said Annie. "Thank you, Annie, I understand." said Rachel. Rachel had dressed in old, raggedy jeans with holes in them, a simple knit top, sneakers, and a hoodie. Annie did Rachel's makeup with what she thought was just enough subtle imperfections. She wanted to give Rachel the appearance of her beauty enhanced by just a little too much makeup, but with a look that could be perceived as having been applied quickly and possibly by a shaky hand. Annie had decided to style Rachel's hair using a top knot with a ponytail. This would go perfectly with her look, and the knot would allow concealment of the small transmitter Connor had given her. She switched it on, then she made sure it was securely fastened and held inside the knot. She examined her handiwork, and the transmitter could not be seen. "Well, I think we're all done." said Annie, combing Rachel's ponytail. "Have a look." Annie added. Rachel stood up and walked over to Annie's floor mirror, which allowed her to see herself from head to toe. Rachel's eyes widened. "Wow, Annie. This is a little scary." she said. "Why's that?" asked Annie. "Because I look so much like I did after I left the Duffields when I was 18! I feel like I'm looking at a mirror into the past!" she exclaimed.

When the three were getting ready to leave, Annie said "I feel so bad. I wish there was something I could do to help." Connor's eyebrows furrowed. "You've given us a place to stay, you've fed us, and you helped Rachel prepare for possibly one of the most important days of her life. You've done more than enough." Connor said. "You know what I mean." Annie said, with a little pretense of pouting. "Thank you for everything, Annie." said Rachel. Rachel gave Annie a long hug and Annie said "You are very welcome. You watch yourself." Rachel nodded. Annie then moved on to Captain and hugged him tightly, looked into his eyes, and said "Y'all, please be careful." Other than when Captain was talking about death, did he ever hear his son sound so serious. "We be careful." Captain said. Lastly, she approached Connor to give him a hug. Connor wasn't even sure who initiated it, or if it was mutual, but the hug he had expected with Annie became a passionate kiss that lasted for almost a minute. It was then followed by a loving embrace. He had that familiar, electrifying feeling run through him once again. This time, he felt even more. *Is this the beginning of love?* he thought. For those few minutes, Connor could think of nothing else. He let go of every worry he had in his life, he let go of the anxiety of their impending operation, he let go of the guilt from surviving his wife, he let go of the guilty feelings of unfounded unfaithfulness, and he was even momentarily oblivious of the fact that his son watching him. When they disengaged their embrace, Connor and Annie looked over at Rachel and Captain. Rachel was smiling from ear to ear. Ever since Captain had been born, there was never a moment when Connor had been away, that he did not look forward to getting back home to see that precious face. He even had a saying that he shared with his son. *If I'm not with you, I miss you.* For the first time in his life, Connor was scared to look at his son's face. After seeing Rachel's huge smile, he looked at his son, terrified at what expression there could be on his face. Connor was relieved to not only see a smile, but Captain exclaimed "Matey! She try to take your bubblegum?" They all laughed, which thankfully lightened the somber mood. Whenever Connor and Captain saw someone kissing, Connor would always ask Captain if one of them was trying to take the other's bubblegum. Captain had cleverly used one of his dad's phrases against him. Connor was thankful that for whatever reason, Captain was not dwelling on his mother at the moment. This would be a discussion for later.

Captain and Connor entered their cubbyhole through the backseat-doorway, carefully pulling the backs of the seats into position and locked them with a latch from the inside. The computer screen provided some light, but they had a small battery-powered lantern with them as well. Rachel got in and started the old car. "Check, check." she said at a normal volume level. "We hear you loud and clear!" Connor yelled from the trunk. Connor wished that it would have been possible for two-way communication, but knew it would have increased the chances of being discovered if Bentley happened to see an earpiece, no matter how small. Rachel pulled out of Annie's driveway, and headed to Duffield's manor. Rachel pulled up to the intercom and put the car in park. She pressed the intercom button and Connor heard the same familiar woman's voice ask "Yes, can I help you?" Rachel's heart sped up, but she maintained an appearance and demeanor of calmness. "I'm here to see Bentley. Tell him it's Rachel." she said. There was a pause of several moments, then the woman said "Mr. Duffield is not available." Rachel bit her bottom lip so hard that she almost brought blood. "Yeah? Well, you tell him I said that was nothing new. He never was available for me unless he wanted something." she said, flatly. She shifted the car into drive and was about to pull away when Duffield's voice came out of the intercom. He simply said "Wait." The powered gates slowly opened. Rachel slowly drove the car through the gate opening. She could see them close behind her in the rear-view mirror. "We're inside of the gate." she said for Connor and Captain's benefit.

Connor's heart started to pound in his chest. Although he had full intentions to do whatever was necessary to help Rachel, he had seriously doubted that Duffield was even going to allow her entry. He held up a thumb to Captain and he returned the thumbs up to his dad. As you would expect of such an expensive estate, the concrete driveway circled around in front of the main house. As Rachel was pulling up toward the veranda, she said "Bentley is standing on the porch with another male." The car came to a stop, she put it in park and then switched off the engine. The Gellars heard the car door open and then close. Connor started the receiver software recording. "Well, I must admit that I thought I'd be seeing you a lot sooner than this. What's it been, about 8 years?" asked Bentey Duffield. "A little over 8." she said. Duffield just nodded. The man beside him silently watched Rachel. "So, who's this? One of your thugs? Did you think you needed a bodyguard for protection from me, a small, young woman?" asked Rachel. The man did not move or change his expression. "There are more ways to hurt someone than by physical abuse." said Duffield. "*You* are telling *me* this? You practically ruined my life with your mind games." said Rachel.

"What do you want, Rachel, money? It's obvious from your car that you don't have any." said Duffield, impatiently. "No, I don't want your filthy money. I want to know why you took me to all of those places, abused me, threatened me, and on top of everything else, tried to make me feel as if it was *my* fault?" Duffield's demeanor did not change. "I have no idea what you're talking about." Duffield said, calmly. "You're a coward and you're scared to admit what you did!" exclaimed Rachel.

Duffield's face turned red. "If you wish to discuss this matter further, then we will do so inside, after you consent to being searched for weapons by Drake, here. Or you can leave. The choice is yours." said Duffield. Rachel walked over to the large man standing next to Duffield and stood spread-eagle facing him. "I can see that you're used to that pose." said Duffield, with a haughty inflection, referring to Rachel's spread-eagle stance. To her surprise and dismay, the very first place Drake reached was the clump of hair on her head. She reached up and grabbed his big arms, but he had already removed the transmitter before she could complain that he was pulling her hair and hurting her. Drake handed the transmitter to Duffield and then patted Rachel down. He found the decoy recorder and car keys. He handed them over to Duffield as well. "Well, what all do we have here?" asked Duffield, looking up at Rachel. Rachel said nothing. "Do you wish to go inside and talk, or do you wish to leave?" asked Duffield. Rachel's defiant demeanor changed and she began to sob. "I need money bad, Bentley. Please help me." she said through her tears. Duffield walked over to her car, opened the door, and tossed the items in her seat, then closed the door back. "Do you want to come in and talk about it?" Duffield asked. Rachel, who was still sobbing, nodded. "Come on in." said Duffield, leading her into his large house. All Connor and Captain could hear were muffled noises from outside of the car. Connor started to feel panicky and was not exactly sure what he should do. "What wrong?" asked Captain. "Daddy's not sure, son. I hope Rachel is okay. I'm not sure what we should do." said Connor.

The inside of the house was just as Rachel remembered. She had a flood of memories that rushed back and tried to overwhelm her, but she held fast. She did have some very pleasant memories and experiences of the life that she had lived here for four years, but the bad ones seemed to cancel out all of the good ones. She knew Bentley to be a creature of habit, and she knew exactly where he was leading her: the library. The room existed as a facade of his knowledge and prestige. But Rachel knew better. Some of her worst memories were in that library, and she knew Bentley knew it as well. As she walked through the house, she remembered there had been quite a few pictures of her on the walls. Unsurprisingly, there were now none. Once they had entered the library, Bentley closed the door behind them. He offered for Rachel to sit on the chaise lounge, which she did. He walked over to the bay window and looked out. Although Rachel was completely in control of her emotions, it was easy to remember and dwell on the bad memories that happened in this library. Without even looking at her, he said "So, what were you planning to do, try to get me to incriminate myself and blackmail me for another $100,000? Or more this time?" asked Duffield. Rachel remained silent for a moment and then said "Bentley, I've got a bad problem, and it's *your* fault that I do. It's the only way I can get through life now and still stand to be myself." said Rachel. Duffield walked over and sat down in the chair behind his expensive mahogany desk. "You had a great life here. Was it really so bad?" asked Duffield.

"You abused me! You took advantage of a little girl! You did it here, in this very room, and every time you took me with you whenever you wanted to show off your little girl to your government friends!" Rachel exclaimed. "You liked it! You never complained about what we were doing when we were together, and you certainly never complained about all the lavish gifts you received!" exclaimed Duffield. "I was just a child! I didn't know what I liked or what I was supposed to do! And I was scared of what might happen if I told anyone! Now that I do know, I would gladly trade everything I've ever gotten from you for just a normal life!" exclaimed Rachel. Duffield was silent for a moment. "Well, you're not a little girl anymore. And yet, here you are again, willing to do the same thing you did as a child for money. Only this time, you *do* know what you're doing and you won't be walking away with $100,000. Not when I can buy the same thing you're selling for much, much cheaper." said Duffield. Rachel looked at the floor. "You're a piece of filthy trash." she said, softly. "But a wealthy one." said Duffield, as he stood up from his chair. He walked toward Rachel.

After a few minutes had passed, Connor looked over at Captain. "I worried about Rachel." Captain said. "Yeah, son, that's exactly what I was thinking. Let's get out of here." Connor unfastened the latch that locked the backs of the seats in place and pushed them forward. He and Captain climbed into the backseat and then opened the back door to get out. Connor noticed the transmitter and the decoy recorder lying in the front seat with Rachel's keys. *Can things get any worse?* he thought. As Captain followed Connor out of the car, they found themselves looking at Drake, Duffield's large body-guard. *I guess they can.* Connor thought. He already had a handgun trained on Connor. Connor had made sure to stand between Captain and Drake, but Captain came around Connor and shouted "No shoot my daddy!" As Connor jumped to try to put himself between Captain and Drake, Drake quickly swung his aim from Connor toward Captain. Connor had seen too many perps recklessly discharge their weapon from being surprised. As soon as Drake's arm had begun to move, suddenly his gun flew from his hand and he began to howl in pain. He thought that he had heard the crack of a distant gunshot. Connor wasn't exactly sure what had just happened, but had no doubt that it had just saved their lives. Drake, now only focusing on his pain, used his other hand to try and massage his stinging gun-hand. Connor quickly pulled his own weapon from his shoulder holster. Connor aimed his gun at Drake. "Lay face down and put your hands behind your head." said Connor. The man did as he was instructed. It was slightly comical to see this large thug, lying face down, while whining about his hand. Connor tried the door and found it to be unlocked. He motioned for Captain to walk about a yard beyond the end of Drake's feet. He picked up

Drake's gun and stuck it in his waistband. He reached into his own pocket and retrieved the multipurpose pocketknife that he always carried and then handed it to Captain. "Okay, Captain, just keep this pointed at him, and if tries to get up or even if he starts to move, just keep pulling the trigger until he stops moving." Connor said loudly as he winked at his son. "Okay, Matey." said Captain, winking back at his dad. Connor retrieved one of the large zip ties that was in one of his cases in their secret compartment and secured Drake's hands with it. "Remember, Captain, just keep that pointed at him and if he even moves, just keep pulling the trigger." Connor said. "I will." said Captain, smiling. Drake did his best to remain motionless.

Connor rushed into the Duffield house, looked around, and listened. He heard what sounded like a scuffle and followed the direction of the sound. He arrived at the library door, just in time to hear the fighting sounds subside. He opened the door in the manner he had been trained to do so in the police force, leading with his weapon, and looked in quickly. Rachel was sitting on Duffield's back with his arm twisted behind him. "Well, I guess everything's under control here." said Connor. "It sure is. This man invited me into his house to talk and then tried to have his way with me. So, I took him down." said Rachel. "I invited you into my house and *you* attacked *me!*" screamed Duffield. "And you . . ." Duffield directed his comments to Connor. ". . . you entered my home *without* being invited in! You're trespassing! You have *nothing* under control!" he added with a loud whine. Rachel pulled out her cellphone and brought up the sound recorder application. She pressed play. Rachel had started recording the moment she had entered Duffield's house. The recording had documented everything that he had said, including the moment when he had just tried to attack her. Duffield, who had his head raised up off of the floor, just dropped it. "How did you hide it to keep Drake from finding it?" Connor asked. Rachel's eyes narrowed, and she just looked at Connor with a reticent and questioning look on her face. "Never mind." he said. She released Duffield's arm and climbed off of him. "So, Duffield, are you sorry for what you've done or just sorry you've finally been caught?" asked Connor. Duffield stood up to see Connor had a gun pointing at him. "I'm just sorry Rachel left when she turned 18." he said with contempt. "Open the front gate, dirtbag." instructed Connor, as he motioned toward the library door with his gun. Duffield led them to the front door where there was a panel on the wall with the intercom, the gate control, and other security settings. He complied with Connor's request and pressed the gate button. "You don't realize who you're dealing with." said Duffield, calmly. "I think I've got a pretty good idea." said Connor, as he motioned for him to go outside. He did so, with Connor and Rachel following him out.

Captain was still standing at Drake's feet, who was still face-down on the concrete, practically as motionless as a statue. "Okay, you can get up now, big boy." Connor said to Drake, as he gripped the man's bound hands and helped him up off of the concrete. Drake looked back at Captain who was still pointing the pocketknife at him. "Oh yeah, hand me my pocketknife, Captain. I wouldn't want it to go off and shoot anyone." said Connor. Captain and Rachel giggled. Drake looked down with embarrassment and shook his head slowly. Connor dialed the number for the FBI contact that Captain Lester had given him. A few minutes later, there were several black SUVs coming up Duffield's driveway. Everyone gave their reports and versions of the incident. Rachel's phone recording file was transferred over to one of the FBI agent's devices. Everyone's contact information was taken down. Duffield and Drake were taken into custody. Rachel, Captain, and Connor were free to go. They piled into the old car and headed back to Annie's place. As soon as the car pulled into the driveway, Annie came running out of the house. She hugged Captain and Rachel with happiness and relief, but for Connor, there was another electrifying, passionate kiss between them. There was no question who initiated it this time: they both did.

| 25 |

Chapter 25: Closures

Connor had been dating Annie for quite a while, and Captain had always been nothing but nice to her. Annie loved Captain very much. One night, when the Gellar men had laid down for their nightly routine, Connor decided that he needed to talk to Captain about his relationship with Annie. While they were eating their snacks, Connor looked over at Captain and said "Captain, I want to talk to you about something." Much like Captain often did, instead of acknowledging the statement, he simply waited for Connor to continue. "You know I love Annie, right?" asked Connor. "I love Annie, too." said Captain. "You know I love Annie a lot like the way I love Mommy?" asked Connor. "You love Mommy?" asked Captain. "Of course, I love Mommy!" exclaimed Connor. "Annie love you and me?" asked Captain. "Yes, Annie loves us both. One of these days, I might want to marry Annie. Would you be okay with that?" said Connor. "Annie love you and me. You and me love Annie. Mommy love Annie. Annie love Mommy." said Captain, with a matter-of-fact tone and took another bite of yogurt. Connor felt like the bottom line was that Captain was okay with Connor and Annie just as long as *everyone* loved *everyone*. Connor felt in his heart as if this was true.

The next day, Connor had a surprise for Captain when they arrived at the office. Connor had the logo for his business changed. The door now read *Gellar & Son Investigative Services*. There was a logo of a pair of angel wings above their business name. "Me?" asked Captain, as he pointed at the word *Son* on the glass door. "Yes, that's you, buddy. The best partner anyone could ever have." said Connor. "The angel wings is Mommy?" asked Captain. "They sure are." said Connor. Captain smiled and gave his dad one of those powerful squeezes that he sometimes gave when he was really, really happy. They were the best hugs, but if you were blessed enough, and strong enough to receive one, you were thankful that you had a skeleton to protect your vital organs. After their embrace, Captain asked "Annie not on there?" Connor smiled. "No, Annie's not on this. Annie understands that Mommy will always be a part of you and me, and will always be in our hearts. Annie is very happy with this special thing to honor Mommy's memory." said Connor. Captain nodded in understanding. The Gellar men entered the office. No coloring pages for Captain today. Connor had a lot of paperwork to catch up on. He was also going to teach Captain how to help with some of the office duties. Connor knew there were going to be some things that Captain would not be able to do. But most importantly, he knew there were a lot of things that he *could* do.

That evening, the Gellars, along with Captain's girlfriend, Katrina, met the Brysons, Rachel and her boyfriend, Francis and David, Annie and Mrs. Peterson at *The Torrenceville Taste* for a meal of camaraderie, thankfulness, and celebration. They were all seated at a large table that had been created by putting smaller ones together. The celebration was mostly due to the fact that Bentley Duffield would never breathe free air again. Much like life, Connor's scheme to take Duffield down had not worked out even remotely as he had planned. However, Rachel's foresight in hiding her cellphone had made it successful. The audio recording provided to the FBI was enough for them to launch a full investigation. They had uncovered other evidence in Duffield's home, including Duffield's own recordings he had made of the abuse Rachel had endured years ago. The celebration was also a myriad of other blessings. Although any minute life can send you into an unsuspecting tailspin, which can turn it up-side down and sideways, it seemed this evening, everyone had something to either celebrate or be thankful for. Rachel had gotten some justice, some closure, and a new lease on life. She had so many job offers based on her criminal justice degree, that she had not yet decided which path to take. Her boyfriend, Keith, was a uniformed police officer and seemed to be a really nice man. She had friends that truly forgave her for the terrible things that she had done.

Not long after Annie's discussion with Connor about Mrs.

Peterson, when he and Captain had first come to town, she had reached out to Mrs. Peterson and befriended her. She had cleaned up her home and gotten it back to a reasonable order. She had begun taking her on weekly trips to the supermarket and trips to the doctor or pharmacy whenever she needed to go. Annie had even brought her to the restaurant with her from time to time, where she could spend some time around other people and enjoy a lunchtime meal on the house. The celebration dinner was the first time Rachel and Mrs. Peterson had seen each other in over 12 years. Connor thought they were going to need a boat to navigate through the restaurant from all of the tears shed from being reunited and the reconciliations. Although they were not blood kin, from what Connor could see from Rachel and Mrs. Peterson's interactions, it looked as though Annie's good Samaritan deeds were going to get subsidized by the reunification of a grandmother and a granddaughter. Daniel was now off of suspension. He had completely recovered from his gunshot injury, and his relationship with his wife was stronger than it had ever been. Connor knew Sandy Bryson had to be *somewhat* uncomfortable at a social gathering with not only her husband's former mistress-of-sorts and the same woman that had shot and nearly killed him. But Sandy knew about Rachel's past and the fact that it had been a major contributor to her mental illness. Not to mention, Sandy Bryson was a strong, classy, Christian woman, and had a very forgiving heart.

Francis announced that David had received a new surgical treatment for his Parkinson's and was having great success with it. Many of the symptoms that had plagued him were either gone or greatly reduced. As with many things in this life, however, the effects of the treatment were not permanent. They had hope of him being more like his old self for at least several years. The doctors had told him to enjoy his improved quality of life while he had it, as there was no guarantee how long it would last. As he and Francis listened to the group's recounting of the events at Duffield's manor, David's interaction with the group left no indication that he even had the disease. Annie, of course, was not working at the restaurant on this evening, as she was also enjoying her own celebration. Through Connor and Captain, she had even more wonderful friends. She had a loving boyfriend that had an even more loving son. She hoped that one day, they could be a family. Katrina was thankful to have Captain as her loving boyfriend. Just as Captain knew that Down syndrome made him have some differences, Katrina also realized the same thing about herself. She felt blessed to be among a group of friends that was not only accepting of her, but actually looked into her eyes and spoke directly to her and didn't talk around her in the third person. They acknowledged her sentience and she saw that everyone treated Captain the same way that they treated her: like a human being.

Captain, being such a loving person, was not difficult to please when it came to being thankful. It made him the happiest when he saw that everyone else was happy, getting along, and enjoying themselves. He had a special way of brightening the day of people he knew and complete strangers alike. Connor looked around the tables at his son and all of his friends, eating, talking, smiling, and laughing. They were all practically family now, brought together by a series of misfortunes and tragedies that had started 14 years ago. Although he also had a special saying of *When Captain's Happy, Matey's Happy,* the reverse saying of the special shirt his son had made for him, he had learned from his son to always try to expand the reach of his caring to others. In that respect, he tried to be more like Captain. Connor always hoped that Captain got as much learning from him as Connor received from his son. He had always said that he had dreams come true that he didn't even know he had. He will always remember how Alexis had said that people were different, and he had learned just how true that was. As Connor was looking around the table at everyone, he found Daniel looking directly back at him.

Daniel stood up and walked up behind Captain, who was sitting between Connor and Katrina. He pulled something out of one of his pockets, coiled it down on the table next to Captain's plate, and then clapped both Gellar men on their shoulders. Captain looked next to his plate to see a simple ball chain necklace with a single decoration attached. Captain then looked up at Daniel and said "Thank you, Daniel." as he picked up the necklace to look at it. Daniel winked at him and then walked back to his seat and sat back down. Connor noticed that on the ball chain necklace hung a single, long shell casing. Captain pulled his magnifying glass out of his pocket and looked closer at the shell casing. The back of the shell casing had a set of numbers, indicating the caliber. Captain turned the shell on its side, and saw some text that had been inscribed. *This one was for you, Captain. Love, Daniel.*

Captain looked at his dad who had been watching him examine the shell. They both looked over at Daniel, who was now busy eating and talking to his wife. Connor felt tears welling up in his eyes, but he forced them back. He thought about the distant shot at Duffield's manor that had disabled Drake, and most likely had saved their lives. He thought about the fact that Daniel, in spite of everything he stood to lose, had come to Duffield's and had hidden somewhere on the grounds. There was no elaboration of Drake's damaged handgun by the FBI. Connor had no doubt if they would have investigated it and a bullet would have been found, it would have been a perfect match to the casing on Captain's new necklace. Captain dropped the chain over his head and pulled the shell casing down straight in front of him. He then slipped his magnifying glass back into his pocket. Things and people aren't always as they appear at first glance. Sometimes you might be surprised at what you might find if you only take a little more time to investigate. And sometimes, you may see things just a little bit differently, through the hand glass.

"Be ye therefore merciful, as your Father is also merciful.
Judge not, and ye shall not be judged: condemn not, and ye
shall not be condemned: forgive, and ye shall be forgiven."

(Luke 6:36-37)-

AFTERWORD

I hope you enjoyed the story. Although this is a work of fiction, the character *Captain* is based upon my real-life son, as pictured on the cover, who has Down syndrome. The nicknames *Captain* and *Matey* are also real. Most of the lifestyle interactions between Captain and Connor are also based upon the real interactions between my son and I. Space showers? Very real, and so is the thank you card pictured in this book that he made for me in 2009.

I pride myself on doing factual research when writing fiction. Regardless of how fantastic the circumstances may be, I try to include scientific facts that can open up doors of many realms of possibilities for things that can *and do* happen in real life, but also make the reader truly believe that *anything* is possible, even if the subject matter is ultimately fiction, and *almost* unbelievable.

In this story, I touched on many real-life subjects and situations and I'm sure most readers are able to relate to at least one of them. I can tell you very quickly that **all of them** have impacted my own life in one way or another. I know that you can find almost anything on the internet these days, but I would like to thank all of the following organizations for allowing me to reference them for your convenience, should you need help or information on any of the topics we addressed:

Childhelp® National Child Abuse Hotline:
1-800-4-A-CHILD (1-800-422-4453)
Childhelp.org®

National Down Syndrome Society®:
800-221-4602
www.ndss.org®

Substance Abuse and Mental Health Services Administration (
SAMHSA):
1-800-662-HELP (4357)
WWW.SAMHSA.GOV

American Parkinson Disease Association®:
(APDA®)
800-223-2732
www.apdaparkinson.org®

American Cancer Society, Inc.®:
1-800-227-2345

Thank you to our men and women in the police and armed forces who keep us safe and thank you to our first responders who are there when we call 911.

And thank you, reader, for reading my story . . .
Chad Gunter